RIDDLE
OF
DARKNESS

M. MALENGA

Copyright © 2018 Mubita Malenga

All rights reserved.

ISBN: 0999194658
ISBN-13:978-0-999-1946-5-2

DEDICATION

Mother.
Sisters.
Brother.
Father.

RIDDLE OF DARKNESS

A Myrtle Jenson Mystery

CHAPTER 1

"The Day my Mother was Kidnapped, we all became Vampires."
This was the title of the most recent performance to come
to town. A shameless attempt to capitalize on the vampire
craze is what one local newspaper labeled it. The other
town newspapers printed reviews that were a lot more
complimentary. The vampire-themed show was quite
successful. Each performance played to a full house,
however, if you ask any of the town residents directly most
will not willingly admit to going to see it. This is strange
seeing as somebody had to buy all of those tickets. Last
week's vampire excitement has subsided and the town
eagerly awaits opening night of the next production that
has rolled into town. A lot of the residents are thankful
this production has nothing to do with vampires. It is a
clear summer night, a beautiful end to the day. There is not
a cloud in sight, perfect for star gazing if one was into that
sort of thing. The night sky shows absolutely no residual
effects of the heavy thunderstorm that rolled through
town only a few hours earlier. The pleasant night air calls

the town's residents outdoors, it is simply too nice to stay inside. Winter has its own charms but nothing compares to the hypnotic energy of early summer. The downtown streets are buzzing with jubilance, even strangers greet each other with smiles as they pass on the street. Everybody seems to be out having fun, everybody except the occupants of the Sunset Auditorium. The Sunset Auditorium is also alive this night, but not with people out for recreation, these folks are hard at work. A giant flyer under the marquee announces the upcoming production to all passersby. The big show date is fast approaching and there are no nights to waste, not even beautiful nights like this.

A dress rehearsal for the Ms. Plus-No Fuss Pageant in Viewgrove is tonight. All of the contestants are present and on their stage marks like they will be on opening night. The dress rehearsal serves to simulate the night of the live pageant and provides organizers an opportunity to make last-minute changes to the elements of the show. The dress rehearsal also allows both the contestants and production crew an opportunity to get a feel for the length of the show. The first run of the rehearsal ends and the contestants grab the opportunity to catch their breath. Until tonight, the pageant contestants have mainly focused on their individual parts. They are not used to being at a rehearsal for this length of time and they are all feeling it. They start to roam the stage during the lighting tests, the initial excitement displayed earlier in the evening is quickly dissipating. The pageant director's energy level is still high, she always gets really excited this close to the show date. With the contestants, stage lights, and music it all seems more real.

The Ms. Plus-No Fuss Pageant is a traveling pageant and coordinating an event in different cities has its challenges. Things do not always go as planned but you adapt and make the best of the situation. An extra grouping of stage lights is putting a lot of stress on the building circuitry. Just as the pageant director is remarking to herself how well the night is going, this happens. The auditorium is suddenly plunged into total darkness. The music continues to play in the background, indicating a blown fuse is to blame and not a block-wide blackout. The Sunset Auditorium is a dated building, a monument to a time before smartphones and tablets accompanied the patrons. The cellular network coverage throughout the theater is spotty at best. Two of the women on the stage chat across to one another for comfort while the others wander the stage in search of those precious signal strength bars that grant access to social media and text messages. The glows from the cell phone screens light up the dark stage like glow sticks at a concert. Two silhouettes are barely visible at the side of the stage. A bloodcurdling scream and punishing thud rudely interrupt all conversation.

An air of panic immediately fills the room. Everybody's heart suddenly beats a lot faster because they are unable to see what happened. Shouts of "what was that?" can be heard repeated in the darkness. The contestants are unable to determine what the noise was but they are hoping it is not what it sounded like. "Please be careful everyone, we'll have this fixed in a minute" offers the pageant director. As if on cue, the auditorium lights come back on, once again flooding the space with light. It takes everybody's eyes a moment to adjust to the sudden flood of light. Pairs of squinted eyes desperately scan the surroundings for the source of the earlier commotion. A few people come to the realization one of the fellow contestants is missing and hurry off to search for her. The search ends abruptly as a contestant exits the side stage and makes a disastrous discovery. One scream turns to a shattering of screams as more people rush over and happen upon the gruesome scene. There she is, the missing contestant, lying lifeless at the bottom of the side stage stairway.

CHAPTER 2

"Calm down ladies, everybody please calm down, give her some space." The Pageant Director frantically rushes toward the side stage. She reaches the fallen contestant's body and nervously presses two fingers against the neck to find a pulse. "Somebody call 911; tell them there's been an accident at the Sunset Auditorium." "Is she dead, she's dead, she looks dead" sobs one of the contestants hysterically. The way the collapsed body is lying there so still makes it easy for the onlookers to assume the worst. The majority of the people present cannot even bear to look. "Does anybody here know CPR?" calls out the pageant director while she tries to get a response from the fallen contestant. Guilt wells up inside her as she thinks back to all of the times she meant to take those CPR classes but put it off. It always seems like something more pressing comes up whenever it is time to take the classes. One of the pageant assistants is trained in CPR, however, she did not make this trip due to a schedule conflict. Now is not the time for self-pity, the emergency has happened and she will deal with it in the best way she can. The contestants take their cues from the director, her calmness is somewhat comforting despite the desperate look of the situation. Unable to find a pulse, or get a response, the director starts to fear the worst. It is obvious that she has taken a very hard fall. The splashes of blood on the floor around the head area are indications of a possible head trauma. To keep from panicking everybody else she continues to put on a brave face and remains in control. She turns to the lighting engineer for help.

"Call 911, tell them to send an ambulance and to hurry," orders the director.

"Nobody leaves until help gets here."

The pageant director needs to make sure nobody else is missing or injured. "Is everybody accounted for, everybody please calmly come to the front of the stage so I can take roll call." Thumbs work to unlock cell phones but the side stage stairway is a dead zone and nobody has any service bars. The lighting engineer sprints off toward the office to dial 911 from a landline. Crowd members offer to move to an area of the auditorium with a reception to dial 911 but the pageant director instructs them not to. Everybody needs to remain accounted for. There is already somebody calling and she does not want to overwhelm the emergency switchboard with multiple calls for the same accident. The pageant contestants are all from out of town and do not know the theater address whereas the lighting engineer is a local resident.

"911, what is your emergency," answers the dispatcher.

"Hello, a young lady is unconscious in the Sunset Auditorium, please send an ambulance!"

"An emergency response team has been dispatched to your location. Can you tell me if she is breathing?" The lighting engineer cannot answer that accurately, "I don't know, I ran as fast as I could to call you, somebody else is with her, please hurry." The lighting engineer hangs up with 911 and sprints back to the others to alert them an emergency response team is on the way. The pageant director acknowledges the engineer's message without looking up, her full attention is on the injured contestant. "Stay with me, help is on the way, it will be okay, help is on the way."

This is a nightmare, by far the worst thing that has ever happened at a Ms. Plus-No Fuss Pageant event. In the past, there have been minor incidents where contestants overexert themselves and need to sit down for a minute. An occasional twisted ankle or a case of dehydration is something they are prepared for, but nothing remotely close to this catastrophe. Everybody gathers around to show support and send prayers. A plea is made that nobody post any of this on social media until there has been a chance to notify the fallen contestant's family. The director looks around for the fallen contestant's cell phone in case the directory lists an ICE number. ICE stands for "in the case of emergency", it is a listing people have in their phone so other people will know exactly who to call in the event the phone's owner is unable to communicate. Everyone associated with the pageant is strongly encouraged to add an ICE number to his or her contact list because you just never know. Only, the contestant's phone is not in plain sight and precious minutes are ticking past. She needs one of the people there to stay with the injured contestant while she retrieves the emergency contact information. The pageant director hastily looks up and chooses the first calm face she sees. "Mr. Goodwill, would you please stay with her for a minute, the paramedics are on the way. I'll be right back, thank you!"

CHAPTER 3

Time slows to a crawl when you are desperately waiting for something. Seconds feel like minutes, and minutes like hours. After what feels like forever, but is really about 7 minutes, the wait is over. A chorus of sirens can be heard growing louder as they approach their destination. A feeling of hope fills the room as the paramedics and police arrive. "This way, please hurry!", shouts the lighting engineer as he motions toward the auditorium double doors. The engineer has been impatiently waiting at the main door of the Sunset Auditorium since he made the 911 call. "She's on the side of the main stage!" yells the lighting engineer as the paramedics rush past him. The double doors to the auditorium swing open and in walks Detective Casper "Zeus" Chaplin, one of Viewgrove's finest officers. The medical emergency professionals are right behind him. Viewgrove is a small community without a large emergency response team. With an ambulance dispatch, a police unit is usually dispatched to assist. The paramedics rush through the auditorium with a great deal of haste. Some of the people in the auditorium are trying to help by lining the aisles and pointing in the direction of the stage. The medical team begins yelling for the crowd to clear the way as they rush toward the side stairs.

"Clear the way, a medical team coming through!"

The crowd parts and clears a path as the paramedics and their equipment rush past them. In these type of situations, seconds count, and the urgency with which the responders are moving is a reminder of that. The paramedics rush into action to try to save the young woman's life. They check her vital signs and begin performing CPR. The mood is tense as the patient does not appear to be responding. The paramedics are not discouraged, they continue to vigorously perform CPR to try to revive her. The responders need to stabilize her so they can transport her in the ambulance. The longer the paramedics work the tenser the room gets. At one point the medical responders charge the defibrillator paddles. The crowd takes another step back as the machine buzzes to life and releases a high pitch beep to indicate charging is complete. Clear! They perform this task two more times. After each round, stopping to check for any signs of life. They do their very best to revive the contestant but their attempts are unsuccessful. The frantic activity stops, they pronounce her dead and inform the lead detective.

The crowd watches in shock as the paramedics cover the body with a white sheet and load it onto a nearby gurney. Gasps of horror can be heard throughout the room. The mood is extremely somber and some of the other contestants begin to sob as the grief overwhelms them. The initial bubble of hope created by the arrival of the paramedics has burst, all of the air has been let out, and the mood in the room is completely deflated. The lead medical team member on site advises Detective Chaplin they need to get the body back to the mortuary. It appears the contestant died from the impact but an autopsy would need to be performed to be one hundred percent certain. The paramedics prepare the body for transport by dressing it in a black body bag. Upon learning the paramedic's news, the detective turns to address the small gathering that has been watching the paramedics work on the former contestant. He gathers himself for a second before getting the crowds' attention. This part of his job is never easy and has not become easier over the many times he has been forced to perform it. What are the right words to say to a room full of strangers about one of their friends or family members that you do not know? No amount of training can truly prepare you for the reality of looking out into the eyes of a crowd of mourners for which this could be the worst day of their lives. Detective Chaplin ends his short statement by encouraging the crowd to disperse so the police can preserve the scene.

The crowd is slow to react to the detective's request. They continue to hover close to the body. Detective Chaplin places a call to the local morgue and requests a transport vehicle be dispatched. A few minutes later he gets a call letting him know the transport vehicle has arrived. The Detective makes another plea, more forceful this time, and the crowd parts to create a clear path for the paramedics to remove the body from the auditorium. The Sunset Auditorium doors swing open as the gurney passes through and gets loaded onto the awaiting transport vehicle. All of the flashing lights and gathered emergency vehicles have attracted a small crowd to the Sunset Auditorium parking lot. The small crowd gathered outside the building is looking for answers to what is going on inside the building. Unfortunately for them, the Police are not providing any answers tonight. The small crowd attracts the attention of the local media but they are unable to uncover many details. The Police are not releasing any names until they speak with the family. The Police spokesman is not making any official statements to the media at this time. The story makes it onto the news that night but it is not the lead story and is therefore buried amongst the other news of the day. The only information they are able to report is the paramedics were dispatched to the Sunset Auditorium and the Police are investigating the cause of death of somebody at the auditorium.

CHAPTER 4

Meanwhile, back inside the auditorium, there is more work to be done. "Please everybody, remain calm, my name is Detective Chaplin and I am the lead officer here. There has been a tragic accident here, you have my sincere condolences." The crowd quiets down allowing the Detective to continue. "There will be grief counselors available for anybody that needs them. I'm going to need statements from everybody so, please, nobody should try to leave until I release you. We will not keep you any longer than we need to." His name is Casper Chaplin. They call him Zeus, for reasons that become obvious once he enters a room. He towers well over 6 feet tall with massively broad shoulders and smooth chocolate skin. Even at retirement age, he is still an imposing figure. He was a serious bodybuilder in his younger years before joining law enforcement and continues to impress the young guys in the gym with his bench press capabilities. Retired from bodybuilding, he works out now just to keep in shape. He definitely still fills out a police uniform. Zeus has no desire to compete on the senior bodybuilding circuit, it would require too large a time commitment. He keeps his face clean shaven and sports a short fade haircut. His barber of fifteen years retired earlier that month which forced Zeus to select a new barber. After much trepidation and debate, he settled on a new young guy in the shop. He is trying to be patient with the new barber but has already had to warn him not to give him one of those "young boy" haircuts as Zeus calls them.

As the senior officer on the police force, Zeus is usually the lead detective on crime scenes. Detective Chaplin often serves as the law enforcement expert on jury cases because local attorneys like to draw from all of his years of police experience. Zeus Chaplin is of retirement age but has no interest in retiring. He loves his job and besides, what will he do if he retires, spend all day fishing? No, not Zeus, he needs to stay active. This job gives him a reason to get up in the morning, it keeps him alive and active. Zeus rarely discusses his personal life. Those close to him know he is single and rarely dates. They often try to encourage him to act on his crush on the retired school psychologist that moved into town. They often cross paths at the town courthouse and he has become increasingly fond of her. Viewgrove is by no means a huge metropolis. The life of a detective, even in this town, leaves little time for dating. Tonight's call is a perfect example of how unpredictable the job can be. Detective Chaplin just happened to be the officer on duty when the emergency call from the Sunset Auditorium came through the switchboard. In a small community like this, a detective may find himself out on all types of calls. However, random deaths in the night are not a common occurrence.

Not even the seasoned Zeus Chaplin, with a history of emergency responses, is prepared for this. Detective Chaplin is determined to find the underlying cause of tonight's event. He is delighted the pageant has come to town and hopes to encourage other events to also consider Viewgrove as a possible destination. Zeus has a personal stake in closing this case as quickly as possible.

The town of Viewgrove is quaint. Postcards featuring the local scenery are often mistaken for scenery from other more well-known locations. This is one of those towns few have heard of but most want to revisit once they have experienced it. When people say they are from Viewgrove, the usual response is, what is that close to? It is definitely one of the country's best-kept secrets and most of the residents like it that way. It is big enough to have a few of the big name stores you would find in the big city but small enough to have just as many locally owned stores. Some of the locals agonize over the town becoming too commercial and losing its charm. They worry about the number of visitors that grows every year as more people become aware of their town. There is also a large community of people, like the detective, who would love to see bigger things come to Viewgrove. The truth is tourism has become a great source of income for the town residents and funds a lot of the town's development. The town would probably not survive if it did not change with the times.

In the time that Detective Chaplin has lived in Viewgrove, he has noticed a fair number of the young people graduate and move away because they prefer to live in the bigger cities with more access to modern amenities.

To thrive, a town needs to be able to attract a talented workforce while retaining its own young workers. Viewgrove is not a one-horse town but it does lack some of the conveniences larger cities take for granted. Most of the town's visitors learn about it from traveling on their way to another city. They arrive via the train line that connects Viewgrove with the surrounding cities. The scheduled train layover allows weary travelers a chance to stretch their legs, and browse the local marketplace.

CHAPTER 5

A concerned citizen monitors all of the flashing police and ambulance lights outside of the Sunset Auditorium. She was finishing the last bites of warm pie and ice cream at her favorite diner when all of the commotions began. There is no point in letting a good dessert go to waste, everyone has at least one guilty pleasure and this is hers. Tonight, she was enjoying her favorite, a la mode combination, the sweet pairing of rich pecan pie with coffee ice cream. Her late husband worked second shift but when he got off at night he would often take her out for pie and ice cream. He never understood her taste in pie and ice cream, his favorite was the classic apple pie and vanilla ice cream combination. She was feeling nostalgic so she left her couch and came to Anna's Diner. Summer nights like this seem to stir up the nostalgia more than others. She has found herself at the Diner several times already this season and has even gotten to know the night staff. "That was good as always Barbara," exclaimed the concerned citizen. A large bill is placed on the counter before she steps down from the bar stool and heads toward the exit. The auditorium is just across the street so she leaves her car in the Diner's parking lot and crosses traffic to see what the commotion is about. Viewgrove is not the kind of town where you would expect to see all of this activity on a weekday or any day for that matter. The concerned citizen walks past the parked police car and enters the auditorium. Detective Chaplin looks up and recognizes an all too familiar silhouette approaching.

"Good evening Ms. Jenson, I didn't expect to see you here at this hour, what brings you by?"

"Good evening Detective Chaplin," she replies.

"I saw the commotion from Anna's Diner. What happened here tonight?"

Her name is Myrtle Mae Jenson. Ms. Jenson is an elderly woman, although she rejects that term, and quickly corrects anybody referring to her as such. Although she is no more than five feet tall, she is difficult to miss. Most folks around town recognize her by her natural silver hair that she keeps in a short curly hairstyle. That is her signature look except for on bad hair days, on those days she wears a curly styled wig that closely resembles her natural hair. Myrtle is proud of herself for resisting the urge to color her hair but it was not always an easy decision. There was a time she would not dare let her hair show any grey. Wearing her natural hair color was one of the changes she made when she moved to Viewgrove. Now she prefers a more natural look and wears very little makeup. Tonight she is wearing a mustard yellow blouse that pops against her brown skin. A pair of nondescript blue jeans and sensible black casual shoes completes her outfit. Over her left shoulder hangs a classic style designer handbag, a gift to herself when she retired. She retired from her career as a school psychologist in the big city and now spends her retirement days volunteering and traveling the world with her band of retired girlfriends. Myrtle is somewhat of a local celebrity in town, at least among law enforcement. She has served jury duty on numerous criminal cases, some of them quite high profile. When cases are too well-known in neighboring cities, the attorneys will request the trial be moved to Viewgrove in hopes of getting an unbiased jury. It seems that retired school psychologists who volunteer in the community are popular with attorneys because it is a common occurrence for her to be selected for a jury panel. All of this jury experience has taught Myrtle a great deal about crime scene evidence, suspects, and criminal motives. She invariably proves more perceptive than her fellow jurors. By carefully piecing the clues together and asking astute questions, she successfully manages to reveal the guilty party. After multiple appearances at the local courthouse, her legend has grown, so much that the police officers and security guards know her by name. She has also become friendly with the local law enforcement, including Detective Chaplin. Over time, Myrtle has noticed the list of people that recognize her has grown. She rejects any notion of local celebrity, Viewgrove is a tight-knit community, eventually, you get to know everybody. The Detective explains that they are investigating the death of one of the pageant contestants and are still in the process of determining the cause of death. The plan is to interview everybody to try and piece together what happened.

Detective Chaplin has a theory which he confidently shares with Myrtle.

"The contestant was leaving the stage via the side stairs when the high heel on her shoe broke off."

"The broken heel caused her to lose her footing, it was dark, she missed a step, and fell down the stairs."

"Oh, that is just awful," replies Myrtle.

As it happens, Myrtle sits on the Sunset Auditorium Board and they just updated the lighting to increase safety and prevent potential accidents. "It is so sad," affirms Zeus Chaplin, "We will know more after the medical examiner has a chance to complete his report." Interpreting the Detective's words as an invitation to assist, Myrtle proceeds to immerse herself in the case. She wonders how many of the people saw or heard anything. Myrtle finds Detective Chaplin's theory very plausible. The broken heel stem is still lying in the same spot it landed on the floor. However, the placement of the scuff marks on the stairs causes Myrtle to question the police theory. Closer examination of the stairs reveals scuff marks not only on the tread of the steps, where you would expect but also on the riser. Myrtle positions herself on the stairway landing to better visualize the fall. Visualization is a technique she often used with her former psychology patients. "Visualize to realize" is the rhyme she would recite to them to help them remember. No matter which way she visualizes the fall, it is nearly impossible to leave those type of scuff marks on both the tread and riser while falling forward. The police hypothesis cannot be correct. The more likely answer is the marks were created by the contestant's black heels as she kicked against the steps while falling backward. This is a more plausible explanation for how the scuff marks ended up on both the tread and riser.

Myrtle asks herself, where is the victim's cell phone, young people do not stray far from their cell phones? A quick scan of the room reveals almost everybody is on their smartphones, essentially proving Myrtle's point. She recalls back to a time when you did not have everything available at your fingertips. Back then, if you wanted to know something you had to work for it, you went to the library and researched it. If you were fortunate, your family owned a set of encyclopedias. She can remember getting lost in those encyclopedia pages for hours at a time. It was so much easier to tell who the smart people were back then. The fun of debate is now lost because you can simply look up the answer on your smartphone. She often wonders if people used their brains more back then. As a young lady, she knew all of her friends and family's phone numbers by heart. The children Myrtle worked with when she was a psychologist solely relied on the programmed numbers on their phone and did not know any phone numbers by heart. Myrtle's back-in-my-day moment reminded her of how people used to stop in to visit each other because they could not reach you every second of the day. How different must it be for people who have grown up never knowing a life without the internet and social media? She often worries about the potentially crippling tailspin effect on young people's lives if social media ever went away.

CHAPTER 6

A junior officer produces a camera from a leather carrying case and quickly snaps several pictures of the scene. Detective Chaplin instructs the officer to begin taking witness statements. Once the preliminary interviews are completed, the pageant contestants are free to return to their hotel rooms with special instructions not to leave town or speak to the media. The Sunset Auditorium closes for the night and everybody heads home. Myrtle Jenson is halfway home but something just does not seem right about the series of events tonight. She replays everything she has learned over in her head but cannot shake the uneasy feeling that things are not as they seem. In psychology circles, it could be referred to as intuition. The pageant director had explained how the lights had gone out temporarily, and when they came back on, the young woman was discovered at the bottom of the side stage steps. Nobody appears to have seen or heard anything, on the surface, it seems like just an unfortunate accident. Ms. Jenson serves on the Preservation Board for the Sunset

Auditorium and she knows for a fact the electrical systems were updated just last month so everything should have been working correctly. Other questions enter her mind, are the stairs unsafe, could the Auditorium be liable? She needs to get back in there and look around for possible answers. Unable to resist any longer, and against her better judgment, she turns her car around and heads back toward the Sunset Auditorium.

The majestic Sunset Auditorium looks very different when closed. Myrtle parks across the street and turns off her car. Out of habit, she starts to reach for her purse and glasses, but then decides there is no need to take all of her personal belongings into the auditorium. She leaves everything on the passenger seat and exits her vehicle. After one last glance at the empty street behind her, she uses her Preservation Board key to let herself into the sleeping auditorium. The building is dark and uninviting, it feels spooky and aged. Myrtle has been in the Auditorium hundreds of times but never at this hour, everything seems very different now that she is alone in the quiet darkness. Once inside, she feels a sense of dread and thinks maybe she has made a big mistake in coming back. She seriously considers leaving and returning in the morning when it is nice and bright outside. Curiosity overcomes her, she shakes off those creepy feelings and advances deeper into the darkness of the Auditorium. Myrtle Jenson is not the only one who has decided to visit the Auditorium tonight. Somebody else is lurking around in the dark shadows. Neither of the two parties is aware of the other's presence. Myrtle does not know exactly what she is looking for but she just needs to examine the scene again. She clicks the switch on the flashlight she brought in from her trunk and the beam of light activates. Myrtle is both relieved and thankful the batteries are still good. Armed with this light beam she makes her way down the aisle toward the main stage casting shadows on the walls and furnishings as she goes. She casually shines her flashlight to the side of the stage looking for the steps and startles an unknown figure in the dark. The shadowy figure catches sight of the flashlight beam, stops whatever he or she is doing, and retreats into the darkness. Myrtle approaches the area vacated by the shadowy figure, unaware of his or her presence. The shadowy figure was quick enough to escape the flashlight beam without being detected. Myrtle arrives at the side stage stairs and feels along the wall for the light switch so she can examine the accident scene in a better light. Finding the switch, she flips it several times, but nothing happens. "That's odd," she thinks to herself, "There is a bulb in there, maybe it has blown out." As a puzzled Myrtle turns her attention away from the light switch, a dark figure leaps out from the shadows and assaults her. A vulnerable Myrtle is pushed with enough force to knock the flashlight out of her hand. The blindside attack catches Myrtle completely off guard. The violent force of the attack hurls her small frame toward the wall, she is unable to keep herself from slamming hard into it. Her body collapses to the ground, and she passes out. She wakes up briefly, barely long enough to make out the silhouette of a dark figure escaping up the aisle, before she passes out again.

Myrtle Jenson wakes up fifteen minutes later on the floor with a pounding headache. She is lying on the floor, in the dark, staring up at the lighting fixture in the ceiling. She gropes around in the dark for her flashlight but cannot find it. She is sore all over from the fall and still trying to figure out what happened. She feels the back of her head gingerly before checking the rest of her limbs for damage. The good news is she does not appear to have broken anything. A mini panic comes over her when she realizes her purse is not on her shoulder. She had already begun making a mental list of which credit cards to cancel and when to schedule an appointment for new glasses before she remembered she left everything in the car. Myrtle feels a sense of relief, glasses are expensive and that is a new prescription. She gives herself a quick pep talk, reminding herself she has been through worse and survived. With that consolation, she forces herself to sit up. Positioned with her back against the wall for support, she takes a minute to gather her bearings. The minutes pass, her eyes start to adjust to the darkness and her mind becomes less groggy. Now more alert, Myrtle is able to identify her flashlight lying on the floor. It had rolled just out of her reach after the fall. She picks up the flashlight, clicks the switch but nothing happens. Only then does she notice the flashlight is making a rattling sound, something on the inside is definitely broken. The flashlight either broke from the impact of the fall or her attacker stepped on it on the way out. Whatever it was, the flashlight is no longer any use to her. Her body screams as she pulls herself to her feet. Gathering herself as best she can, she feels her way to the exit, there will be no more looking for clues tonight.

CHAPTER 7

Myrtle's self-examination did not reveal any broken bones; however, she decides to take herself to the hospital emergency room just in case. There is always the chance she has some internal injuries and it is best she catches any issues early. The adrenaline has worn off and she is definitely feeling the full effects of the attack now. The auditorium doors close and lock behind her. The night air feels good even though it hurts if she breathes too deeply. The short painful walk back across the street is almost over. Her parked car is now in view. Anna's Diner is where it has always been but now it feels so far away. Finally, Myrtle reaches her car, it is easy to find because it is the only one left in the deserted parking lot. Myrtle rumbles around in her front pocket and produces her keys. A push of the faub unlocks the car door with a chirp. She opens the door and gingerly lowers herself into the driver's seat. A quick glance over at the passenger seat confirms her purse and glasses are safe and sound right where she left them. She starts the car and allows it to idle for a minute while she decides if she is okay to drive. After a couple of deep breaths, Myrtle feels able to drive so she puts the car in gear and pulls into traffic. A short drive later Ms. Jenson arrives at the Emergency Room. The automatic glass doors start to slide open upon her approach. As the door is sliding open she sees her reflection in the glass. During the struggle in the auditorium, her wig had become crooked. She had not noticed while in her car but now under these bright lights, it was very clear. Myrtle walks right past the on-duty receptionist and straight into the restroom. It was bad enough that she was hobbling in, she sure was not going to speak to anybody with a twisted wig on, who knows what they may think. Her regular hair appointment was not for another two days, she just had to look presentable until then. Myrtle emerges from the restroom with her hair neatly in place and finally checks in at the reception desk. After calmly explaining why she is there, Myrtle is asked to fill out some forms and take a seat. The Emergency Room waiting is surprisingly empty tonight. Warm nights like tonight often encourage people to overindulge which often leads to them doing silly things that land them in the Emergency Room.

Myrtle sinks into a cushioned seat in the empty waiting room. She laughs to herself about how other people might consider what she did tonight something silly, and they could be right because she ended up in the emergency room. If only she had gone home instead of turning around to go back to the auditorium. Perhaps if she had never left the Diner in the first place and gotten involved she would be safe in her bed right now. She has spent her life helping people. Old habits die hard and she is not about to change her ways at this point in her life.

She decided long ago that she would commit herself to helping others. Myrtle was married once, she married her college sweetheart right after graduation. They always wanted children, although they tried for many years they were unsuccessful. As a result, she looked out for everybody else's children like they were her own. The reason she became a school psychologist was to help children. Her husband was killed several years ago. Right after that happened she picked up and moved to Viewgrove in search of a new start. Their retirement plans were drastically changed when he was one of three innocent people killed during a botched bank robbery attempt. Myrtle worked tirelessly to help bring his killer to justice. Her efforts were unrewarded and the killer got off with a light sentence. Myrtle was devastated and embarrassed by how little she knew about the legal system. The case gave her a new purpose and drive. She was already a trained psychologist but she felt like she needed more. So, she read books, volunteered with law enforcement, took classes, and did everything she could think of to sharpen her crime-solving skills. The majority of her life was dedicated to helping children, but whatever years she has left will be dedicated to putting criminals behind bars.

Thirty minutes go by and the attendant brings Myrtle Jenson into a room to see a nurse who asks her to describe her pain level on a scale of 1 to 10. The nurse takes her blood pressure and sends her back to the waiting room area. Thirty more minutes go by, the exact same thing happens, and she is back again in the waiting room. Thirty more minutes go by and Myrtle has not been called back to see the doctor yet. The Emergency Room waiting area is still empty and she has not seen anybody leave, nothing has changed in the hour and a half she has been there. She walks up to the front desk attendant and informs her she has changed her mind about waiting to see a doctor.

"Ms. Jenson, we were just about to call you," states the front desk attendant.

"Don't bother," replies Myrtle.

The front desk attendant tries to convince Myrtle to reconsider and come back to see the doctor but with no success. Myrtle may be a senior citizen but she is tougher than she looks. Once she makes her mind up there is no stopping her. She makes a deal with the front desk attendant, "If I still feel lousy in a couple of days I'll call my doctor and schedule a visit." On her way out, Myrtle tells the front desk attendant, "I'll take two aspirins and call you in the morning, good night or should I say good morning." With that said, she gingerly exits the Emergency Room as the automatic glass doors close behind her. The crisp morning air feels good against her face. She inhales deeply on her walk back to her car. Myrtle unlocks the car door and eases into the bucket seat. "Home George," she says as she starts the engine and heads home to the healing powers of her own bed. It was a short drive home through the empty town streets. The route is so familiar to Myrtle that she did not even remember any details of the ride home, it was like the car was on autopilot. Her body had been throbbing earlier but now she barely noticed. Her mind is too focused on what had happened hours earlier to waste precious energy on the physical pain. She keeps replaying the moments right before the attack over in her mind. Feeling less emotional now, she replays the event once again but this time through her psychology lens. Was this a case of fight-or-flight? Perhaps she had cornered her attacker and triggered a survival reaction resulting in the assailant knocking her to the ground so he or she could escape? It was a few minutes before Myrtle looked up and realized she had made it home. She glanced at the glowing car clock and tried to guestimate how long she has been just sitting there in her driveway. "Come on Myrtle", she murmurs to herself, "take a hot bath and go to bed, you've had a long day." She was bent in several places but she was not broken. Her intuition is telling her tonight's attack on her is somehow connected to what happened earlier to the pageant contestant. She was now more determined than ever to find the connection between the two incidents at the Sunset Auditorium.

CHAPTER 8

The next morning Myrtle contacts Detective Chaplin to advise him of the attack the previous night. In hindsight, she probably should have reported the incident right after it happened but there is nothing she can do about that now. All she can do now is suffer the safety lecture she knows will come from Zeus Chaplin. She knows he only fusses because he cares.

"Oh, my goodness Ms. Jenson, are you okay?" asks the concerned Detective.

"I'm fine Detective, just a little sore, everything hurts but my feelings," answers Myrtle.

"Somebody did not want me snooping around that auditorium last night."

Zeus Chaplin is relieved to learn Myrtle is not seriously injured. Now that she is okay, for the most part, he wastes no time and fusses at her about safety. The only way she can get him to stop is by promising not to go off on her own like that again. Satisfied that he has fussed enough, and to Myrtle's relief, he agrees to drop the subject. Zeus's last question is an attempt to make Myrtle feel better, "You didn't get sauce all over my crime scene, did you?" Myrtle laughs, "No sir, my bottle of hot sauce is safe in my purse, I didn't take my purse in with me." The fact she carried hot sauce in her purse had become an inside joke between them. Myrtle loves to remind him that she was doing this before it became trendy. Zeus advises her that due to the attack he will be back at the Sunset Auditorium that morning to process the scene for clues and possibly conduct more interviews.

"I need you to either come down to the police station or meet me at the Auditorium later."

Detective Chaplin needs the details of Myrtle's attack so he can file an official report on her behalf. She agrees to meet him in the auditorium to make a statement for his report. The real reason she wants to meet with the Detective is to get an update on the pageant case. The Ms. Plus-No Fuss Pageant is holding another brief rehearsal since the last one was canceled due to the accident. The local grief counselor will also be at the Sunset Auditorium to assist anybody that needs it. Myrtle arrives at the auditorium and wastes no time in getting down to business.

"Detective Chaplin, have you heard anything from the Medical Examiner?" she asks.

"Actually, I did hear something back," responds the Detective.

He had just gotten off of the phone with the Medical Examiner's office right before taking Myrtle's call earlier. The initial Medical Examiner's report shows no signs of exhaustion in the victim. Initially, the cause of death appears to be the impact from the fall. However, simply tripping down those side stairs would not generate enough force to cause death on impact. The Medical Examiner will issue the final report in a few days. The possibility of foul play cannot be ruled out at this time. This case just turned into a murder investigation. In Detective Chaplin's hands are the crime scene photos taken the night before. "Detective, do you mind if I look at those?" Myrtle studies last night's photos with the same tenacity as she studies the crime scene photos on jury cases. She has an uneasy feeling about the tragic event. Zeus Chaplin has been a detective a long time and all of his experience is telling him there is something more to uncover here. Myrtle listens carefully to the Detective's report without interrupting him.

"Do you mind if I hang around here today, I could be of some assistance?" asks Myrtle.

"I don't know, the police will find and arrest your attacker if that is your interest here."

"Detective, a murderer could be roaming free, bringing him or her to justice is my interest here!"

"Alright Myrtle, your insight could be valuable, just remember this is a police matter."

"Oh, you'll get no trouble out of me Detective, I'm more than happy to follow your lead."

"I'm holding you to that Myrtle, you need to clear all actions through me."

The desk officers at the police station run preliminary backgrounds on all of the people the Detective considers persons of interest. These officers are working on short notice so the information they have gathered so far is only what they could find on the internet. Full backgrounds and follow-up information will take a police force of this size a little more time. Detective Chaplin will still have to rely heavily on his deduction skills in order to identify any possible suspects and motives. Zeus has not seen anything this serious in the sleepy town of Viewgrove for a very long time. He is by no means naïve, crime can happen anywhere. However, he quietly hopes to himself that he will not see anything this serious for a long time after this. He left the police force in the big city to get away from heinous crimes like this. Years of working violent crimes in the big city had started to wear on him and he needed a change. He needed to believe in the goodness of people again. Viewgrove was such a contrast to what Detective Chaplin had been used to. He almost put in for a transfer after his first week in town because the pace just felt way too slow for him. He was not used to policing in this type of environment but in time he grew to like it and then love it. People here seem to genuinely care about their community. The town has provided him just the therapy he needed and restored his faith in peoples' good nature. Detective Chaplin cannot even imagine living anywhere else, this is his home now.

CHAPTER 9

Detective Chaplin and Myrtle Jenson's first interview is with the Ms. Plus-No Fuss pageant's director. One of the first people to reach the contestant after the incident was the Pageant Director so they are both very interested in what she may have seen or heard.

"Good morning ma'am, I'm Detective Chaplin, and this is Ms. Jenson."

"Good morning Detective Chaplin and Officer Jenson," replies the Director.

Zeus Chaplin explains how Ms. Jenson is not a police officer but is assisting the police with the investigation. The Pageant Director nods her head at him in acknowledgment. He asks if they could have a few minutes of her time? "Of course, please, anything you need," comes the answer. Zeus thanks her and begins with the most obvious question. "Would you please state your name for the record ma'am?" The Pageant Director's face lights up. "Ma'am, I'm not old enough to be a ma'am," she snaps, "Oh, no offense Miss. Myrtle." Everybody knows that attaching a miss to the front of somebody's name is an acknowledgment that they are older, so old that you do not feel comfortable addressing them by just their first name. Most people would not consider this a big deal, however, most people do not have the same level of distaste that Myrtle has for being pointed out as elderly. If she did not have Myrtle's full attention before, she certainly does now. "Why would I be offended?" asks a clearly offended Myrtle. The Pageant Director ignores the question but keeps looking over, she is trying to figure out why the name Jenson sounds so familiar. To boost local interest in a new town, the Director tries to recruit a few local celebrities to be on the judges panel. Myrtle had received one of these requests to be a pageant judge but had declined it due to a previously scheduled engagement. In a strange twist of fate, she canceled that same engagement to focus on this case. A knowing look comes over the Pageant Director's face as she remembers why that name sounds familiar. After a short awkward silence, the Director continues. "My name is Wendy Ross aka Sweet Mama Marmalade!" She explains that she owns and runs the pageant. Although she introduced herself as Mama Marmalade, most people just know her as Ms. Marmalade now. She knows Zeus and Myrtle are both thinking, she has seen that puzzled look hundreds of times before. Why go by Ms. Marmalade as opposed to Wendy Ross? Before they can even think to ask, she beats them to it. "As you can probably imagine, it is a little harder to get sponsorship when your last name is Ross, I can't tell you all of the extra questions you get," she offers. "Potential sponsors hear the name Ross so they accept the request for a meeting, most likely with hopes of working with a more famous Ross. However, they automatically think I have money. They immediately start treating me like I'm heir to some music fortune and don't need sponsorship." Detective Chaplin sympathizes with her struggle, whereas Myrtle is not moved in the least. "Are you by chance an heir to a fortune?" asks a curious Detective. "Ha, there's no relation. No way, I wish, I'm just Mama Marmalade. I'ma fake it til I make it!" answers an animated Ms. Marmalade. "I've got big dreams, one day this pageant will be a big deal, you wait and see, you'll be watching it on television."

Ms. Marmalade is an ambitious woman. She built the Ms. Plus-No Fuss pageant from nothing and fought hard to make it what it is today. Securing sponsorship for the pageant is not always easy due to pre-conceived notions of plus-size pageants. There are people out there who do not believe anybody would want to see a plus-size pageant. Despite all of the obstacles, including being on the brink of bankruptcy, she is able to push through and successfully put on the pageant every year. Ms. Marmalade is no stranger to struggle and is used to people underestimating her. She has a me-against-the-world attitude and uses any perceived slight as motivation. Ms. Marmalade takes the fact that Myrtle Jenson declined her invitation to be a judge as an insult against her pageant, and will use it to fuel herself. Myrtle's presence is putting the interview subject on guard. If Detective Chaplin had known about the declined invitation he might have anticipated the tension and interviewed Ms. Marmalade alone. The Detective definitely would have received a warmer reception. As it stands he has no idea what the origin of the tension is. All he knows is that something is going on between those two. Just as he is thinking of the best way to smooth out the tension they are back at it again. "We were so excited when we learned the Sunnyset Auditorium decided to host the pageant, we never expected anything like this," states Ms. Marmalade. "Nobody ever does Miss," adds a sympathetic Zeus Chaplin.

"I think you meant to say Sunset Auditorium," chirps Myrtle.

"Huh, what are you talking about?" asks Ms. Marmalade.

"I know the name but I've been calling it Sunnyset Auditorium the whole time, it's a habit now."

"I'll call it what I want to call it, you know what auditorium I mean," snaps an irritated Ms. Marmalade. "Do you speak French, Lady Marmalade?" asks Myrtle rhetorically. Ms. Marmalade shoots her the dirtiest side eye and just as she is about to respond, Detective Chaplin breaks back into the conversation to ease the tension and get the interview back on course.

CHAPTER 10

"Ms. Marmalade, I understand you are the one who discovered the body?" questions the Detective. "Yes, I did, she was in the side stairway. After the paramedics were called I left Porsha with somebody for a few brief minutes while I went to retrieve her emergency contact information."

"Did you say you left the body after discovering it?" asks Zeus.

"Yes, I did. It doesn't make a lot of sense now that I think about it but at the time I was concerned with contacting her family as soon as possible. Even though I came right back, I should have stayed with her the whole time, I regret that decision." Detective Chaplin needs to find out more about the victim. He kindly asks the Director to provide the victim's name. Ms. Marmalade's demeanor returns to calm, "Her name is Porsha Jones," she replies sadly. "I was so excited to have her participate in this year's pageant. Porsha holds a few other pageant titles so she's a big deal in the pageantry circles." Ms. Marmalade was exactly right. Porsha Jones normally competes in pageants a lot bigger and more prestigious than this one. There was great excitement and disbelief when she actually accepted the invitation to participate in the Ms. Plus-No Fuss Pageant. Ms. Marmalade explains further, "Porsha participating in your pageant instantly boosts the perception, she had so much life yet to live." She offers to turn over Porsha's pageant application and emergency contact information if it would be useful. "Yes, please submit whatever information you have on Ms. Jones that would be helpful."

Zeus Chaplin wants to know if she noticed anything out of the ordinary in the past week, fights, arguments, perhaps strangers hanging around the venue? "No, not at all, everything seemed normal," Ms. Marmalade replies. "I spoke to Porsha just the other day and she was her normal happy self, she told me she felt confident about her chances of winning. She was looking forward to performing her spoken word monologue." One of the highlights of the Ms. Plus-No Fuss Pageant is the talent portion. The talent portion is filled with several different kinds of performances and gives the contestants an opportunity to express their individuality. Some contestants choose to sing songs while others choose poetry, dance, or other forms of expression. "Would you say Porsha was a very competitive person?" asks the Detective. "Sure, all of the women are a little competitive. I would not say she was more competitive than the other contestants were. Porsha was very talented and heavily favored this year. It is no secret she was my most talented contestant; I would not have been surprised if she had won the pageant crown this year. I never shared this with the other contestants or judges, but it was her contest to lose." Myrtle has been sitting quietly the entire time due to the earlier tension between her and Ms. Marmalade. If she had continued on, in the same way, the Detective would have asked her to leave. She feels like she has waited an appropriate amount of time and seizes an opportunity to inject herself back into the conversation. "Were there any tensions between Porsha and the rest of the girls?" asks Myrtle. "This pageant is about supporting women to enhance their well-being, not about drama," answers Ms. Marmalade. "The pageant participants have the chance to enhance their love for community service through volunteering and supporting charitable causes. The participants also develop their public speaking and performance skills through the talent portion of the pageant."

At its core, the Ms. Plus-No Fuss pageant is about boosting self-esteem and sisterhood. In all of the years, there has not been a lot of conflict between the contestants. The pageant contestants usually do not know each other but bond through the shared pageant experience. Ms. Marmalade does not recall any fights or arguments, but she does recall a rehearsal, about a week ago, where three non-contestants were present in the audience. She shares the information with the Detective. "Is that the kind of information that's important?" she asks. Zeus nods and advises that information could be very useful. "Do you know any of these three people personally?" She thinks back for a minute. "No, I don't, they're all strangers to me", answers Ms. Marmalade. She points out that those same three people are actually in the auditorium today, and she would be happy to point them out. "Please let me know if there is anything else I can help you with. I've already advised my assistant Jenna to provide you with any information you might ask for. Please feel free to see me or her for any pageant information you need." Detective Chaplin believes Ms. Marmalade when she says she takes pride in being very customer oriented and strives for both patrons and contestants to have the best experience possible. A tragedy like this could be enough to postpone or even cancel the show. This is not the kind of publicity the show is seeking.

"May I ask you another question Ms. Marmalade?" asks Myrtle.

"Sure, what's your question?"

Myrtle proceeds, "Did you find a cell phone on the victim when you discovered her body that night?" Ms. Marmalade considers the question. "No, I don't recall seeing any cell phone, I looked for it briefly right after I found Porsha so I could call her parents but I didn't see it, is that important?" Myrtle gathers her things and prepares to stand up. "Thank you for your time ma'am," and with that Myrtle exits and leaves the Detective to conclude the interview.

CHAPTER 11

"Detective, Detective, can I ask you a few questions?" Zeus Chaplin looks around slightly confused as he tries to establish where this voice is coming from. "Over here Detective", comes the voice again. The owner of this mystery voice is Davina Roberts, a local news reporter. "Davina Roberts from the Viewgrove Gazette." Zeus is disappointed to learn a reporter has made their way into the auditorium. A news story is not what he needs right now, he was hoping to buy a little more time. Once these stories hit the evening news the public expects the crimes to be solved in forty minutes like on television. The police had kicked a news reporter out of the Sunset Auditorium last night, Zeus wonders if this is the same one? Davina Roberts actually is the same news reporter, today is her second day on site following the story.

"What are you doing here?" asks Zeus.

"I'm working, just like you are Detective."

"This is my second day here, can you give me an update on the progress of the case?" asks Davina. "Update?" repeats the Detective, "No, I don't have any statements for you at this time." He wonders how she even learned about the story so quickly? Everybody knows all reporters have sources that tip them off to news stories all of the time. This story was going to get covered at some point, there were just too many people involved for it not to get leaked. Davina takes another shot, "Do you mind if I interview some of these people?" Detective Chaplin really does not have time for this right now, "Yes, I do mind Davina, I don't want you making this thing bigger than it is, and we don't need any headlines right now." An offended Davina defends herself, "I would never do that Detective, I only report the facts, and I do not sensationalize things!"

Davina can read the anguish on Zeus's face so she proposes a deal. In exchange for exclusive interviews, once the case is resolved, she agrees not to go public with any case details she learns today. Zeus Chaplin is reluctant to accept any such offer, this could set a bad precedence. Who knows how many more reporters are inside the Sunset Auditorium and how many more deals he will have to make before the day is done. He orders one of the officers to guard the auditorium front door with strict instructions not to allow any more press members inside. "You're just not going to quit are you Davina?" replies Detective Chaplin, finally. "Okay, we have an agreement, keep this a non-story for now and we have a deal." They both know that Viewgrove is a small town so there is bound to be some talk around town regarding what happened here. As much as the Detective would like to think everybody would be mindful not to release information, he knows there will be some information leaked out. The Detective turned to walk away when he heard another request from Davina Roberts.

"What is it Davina, I have work to do?"

"Do you mind if I interview the Pageant Director?" she asks.

"Fine, just make sure you don't release any pertinent details," and with that, he ended their conversation. Davina is pleased though, she does not want to press too hard and end up being escorted out of the auditorium. As it stands right now, she is the first and only reporter on the inside and that is how she wants it to remain. There were a few reporters outside the auditorium but they were being kept out by the police. She quietly makes her way through the auditorium in search of the pageant director Ms. Marmalade. Ms. Marmalade is not easy to track down, Davina has to practically run to catch up with her to request an interview. Davina has to show Ms. Marmalade her press credentials to prove she is really a legitimate reporter with the newspaper before she finally agrees to be interviewed. "I don't want to be talking with just anybody," explains Ms. Marmalade. Davina assures her that the story will make the papers, although deep down she knows she cannot guarantee it. She feels a slight twinge of guilt but she cannot risk the chance of missing out on the story if it turns out to be a big one.

The local reporter toggles through the options on her smartphone, activates the record feature and gently places the phone on the table in front of her. "This is

Davina Roberts, reporting from the Sunset Auditorium where an accident happened last night during a dress rehearsal for the Ms. Plus-No Fuss Pageant. I'm joined by the Pageant Director, Ms. Marmalade. Thank you for taking the time to speak with me Ms. Marmalade. Can you start by giving us some background about the Ms. Plus-No Fuss Pageant?" The Pageant Director opens with a warm greeting and thanks Davina for taking the time to interview her. She is very polished when she needs to be and comes across very likable in interviews. Before answering the question posed, she expresses her sincere condolences to Porsha's family. Ms. Marmalade assures Davina the pageant is nothing but positive, despite the circumstances of their meeting.

The Ms. Plus-No Fuss Pageant has been operating for over half a decade without any issues. Ms. Marmalade was inspired to create the pageant when her local area could not meet her passion for plus-size pageants. The Ms. Plus-No Fuss Pageant is committed to supporting full figured women to enhance and improve their health and well-being. The pageant aspires to build a healthier community through positive networking, building new relationships, motivating personal growth, and encouragement. The home base for the Ms. Plus-No Fuss Pageant is in Tennessee, but on occasion, pageants are held in other parts of the country. Each year groups of talented women compete for the title of Ms. Plus-No Fuss. "Now let me tell you a little bit about my story" volunteers Ms. Marmalade without being asked. She went on to explain how she came from simple beginnings and explained some of her struggles to get to where she is now. She shared how her goal was to grow the pageant into one of the biggest events in the country. Admittingly, Davina had never heard of the Ms. Plus-No Fuss pageant before it arrived in town. However, listening to Ms. Marmalade talk about the pageant's humble beginnings and the mission inspired her. She can relate to some of the struggles of trying to break into an industry and she now finds herself rooting for the pageant's success. Davina Roberts kindly thanks Ms. Marmalade for her time. She picks up her smartphone and ends the recording by signing off, "This is Davina Roberts for The Viewgrove Gazette, signing off for now."

CHAPTER 12

The gravity of what has occurred is getting to be too much for Ms. Marmalade so she steps away for a minute to gather herself. She is no use to her contestants if she is an emotional mess. Before anybody can stop her to ask a question, she slips into the ladies room and locks the door behind her. Just a few moments alone to gain her composure and reapply her brave face, that is all she needs. In this timeout, Ms. Marmalade practices some deep breathing techniques in the bathroom mirror to calm herself. These are the exact breathing exercises she teaches to her nervous pageant contestants. In that moment of solitude, her mind wanders back to how different things were a week ago.

"From the top, this time with the music, get it!" yells Ms. Marmalade. The music comes on and the group starts to move. "No, no, stop, stop the music. Ladies, the pageant is in a week, we need to have this routine down by then," Ms. Marmalade was growing impatient with all of the mistakes. "Some of you are still out of sync with the group. I know it's getting late and I know I'm pushing you hard but I know you can do it". The Director believes in putting on a polished show, if the show falls apart it will not be due to lack of caring. She is a perfectionist who believes in putting on the most professional show possible. "Now, once again from the top, DJ, music please, get it!" she yells, and with that, the bass kicks in and the women work through the routine.

A week ago, all of the contestants were getting more excited by the day. Finally, they would get to display everything they have been working so hard on for the last two weeks. The opening dance routine is a Ms. Plus-No Fuss Pageant staple and is always a crowd favorite. The routine involves all of the contestants and helps to set a mood of unity for the evening. It is important for the show opening to go off without a hitch. The opening number changes every year and pageant patrons look forward to seeing what the opening number will be. The pageant was on the road so Ms. Marmalade did not mind if a few people were in the audience for support. Today she is second guessing that decision along with a few others. Everything had been going as planned and no one could have ever predicted what would happen just a few days later, but here we are. In this moment, all of the hard work and stress feels a little empty. Ms. Marmalade takes a last look at herself in the mirror, applies a fresh coat of lip gloss, and exits the ladies room.

Myrtle Jenson and Detective Chaplin both decide the three audience members are at least worth talking to, if for no other reason than to quickly rule them out as suspects. It could be nothing more than a simple coincidence that these three attended the closed rehearsal. It would not be the first case of right place at the wrong time. Myrtle and Zeus need to be sure either way. The more suspects they can quickly eliminate the better. Zeus takes out his writing pad to record the names of the three audience members that Ms. Marmalade had mentioned. He constantly jots case details down on that pad. Sometimes the details he records will not connect until much later in the case. Perhaps he will use the notes to write his memoir one day, anything is possible.

"No tablet to record those names in Detective?" asks Myrtle.

"No Myrtle," replies Zeus, "I still like to do some things the old-fashioned way."

According to Ms. Marmalade, the first person on the list is one of the pageant judges named Martin Goodwill. The second person is a non-contestant named Sheila Johnson, she happens to be the sister of one of the contestants. The third person is named Roxanne Williams, she is a friend of another one of the contestants. Myrtle wonders what connection these three have to the victim or each other if any at all. Detective Chaplin feels a lot of the time it is the people closest to the victim that are the most helpful in solving these types of cases because they provide some insight into the victim's personality. In this case, he feels it would be difficult for a stranger not to be noticed by a member of the pageant group. However, he is still looking forward to what he may learn from these interviews. Ms. Marmalade has already offered to point out these individuals to him and he is going to take her up on that offer. Zeus stands with Ms. Marmalade as she scans over the small crowd. "Detective," she says, "That's Martin Goodwill right there, the gentlemen in the green shirt over by the exit sign." Zeus turns to see where she is looking. Martin Goodwill has his back turned to them but the Detective locks in on his position as he makes his way through the small crowd toward him. Once he is close enough he addresses Martin Goodwill. "Mr. Goodwill, can you come this way, I'd like to have a word with you." Martin turns around to see who is speaking to him. He cannot think who would be addressing him as Mr. Goodwill here, in fact, most of these people would not even know his surname. He turns and is shocked to see a police officer and what looks like his partner standing behind him.

CHAPTER 13

"Good morning sir, my name is Detective Chaplin, and this is Ms. Jenson. Ms. Jenson is consulting with the police and will be sitting in on this interview." Detective Chaplin is well aware the person who attacked Myrtle could be among the people being interviewed today. He is hoping that allowing Myrtle to sit in on the interviews will rattle the perpetrator and he may be able to connect the two cases. Myrtle is focused more on solving the murder case, although if she is also able to figure out who attacked her it would be a welcomed bonus.

"Would you please state your full name for the record?"

"My name is Martin Goodwill but you can call me Goody."

Zeus asks Goody what he remembers about the night in question. "I already gave the officer my statement last night," protests Goody. Detective Chaplin leans in closer to Goody for effect, "Mr. Goodwill, this is a possible murder investigation, we need to account for everybody's whereabouts!" Point taken. Goody sits up straight and fixes his attitude before he continues. When he speaks again it is with less hostility in his voice, "Okay, okay, give me a second to remember." Goody recalls being in the auditorium the night of the rehearsal, everything seemed to be going fine. He was making notes for a work project he had due the next week and was not paying any attention to the rehearsal. He remembers the sudden blackout. When the lights went out he could not see his hand in front of his face. It seemed like the lights were out forever. The next thing he remembers is hearing a lady scream. Goody apologizes to the Detective for not being much help. Just when it looks like a total loss, Goody offers this, "Come to think of it, I don't remember seeing the one young lady, I think her name is Sheila or the lady that died before the lights went out."

Myrtle finds Goody's last response interesting. There is the problem of language expectancy, meaning in certain situations you would expect to hear certain language used. Goody had a chance to express condolences for the victim or sympathy for the situation. Instead, he provides a detail involving another person without being asked. This violated Myrtle's language expectation for the interview. She asks Goody if he knew the young lady that died, while carefully listening for his response. "No, I just know she was a contestant in the pageant," replies Goody. A disturbing thought suddenly enters his mind, "Hey, this is not going to be in some official record is it, my name is not going to be in the newspaper, is it?" Once again Myrtle does not receive the expected response. "We're not reporters Mr. Goodwill, we're just trying to find out what happened to the girl," she replies to him. Zeus steps back in and asks Goody how he came to be a part of the Ms. Plus-No Fuss Pageant? Goody explains how he met Ms. Marmalade at a volunteer function for another organization they both support. He was interested in the message of the pageant and told Ms. Marmalade he would love to be a part of it if she ever needed any volunteers. Goody is in the running for a promotion at work and figures this type of volunteer activity will look good on his resume. As it turns out, Ms. Marmalade needed a volunteer due to Myrtle declining her invitation. "May I ask you a question Mr. Goodwill?" asks Myrtle. Without waiting for a response, she asks, "Did you notice a cell phone on the victim when you waited with her body last night?" Goody is a little thrown off by the question. "No, I didn't", he finally replies. Detective Chaplin concludes the interview and releases Goody. "Thank you for your time and cooperation Mr. Goodwill."

Detective Chaplin and Myrtle Jenson walk off to a secluded area of the auditorium to get each other's thoughts on the interview. "Well that was interesting", begins Detective Chaplin, "I can't say I can rule him out as a suspect yet." Myrtle agrees with him, based on the interview, she cannot rule Goody out either. Myrtle asks if there is anything additional in the Police research regarding Mr. Goodwill? Zeus begins to read the short report to Myrtle, "His name is Martin Tremaine Goodwill but has been known to go by the nickname Goody." The short research from the police department confirms most of what he has already told them in the interview. The county records list him as unmarried. His driver's license lists his age as thirty-eight. His last known employment is an auditor for a prominent accounting firm. There were a few details that Goody did not volunteer. There is a police report from three years ago. Mr. Goodwill was charged with stalking and violating a restraining order. The accuser claimed Mr. Goodwill had a plus-size fetish and ignored repeated requests to leave her alone. The situation escalated into an altercation. The pending charges were dropped when the defendant agreed to a plea bargain. His driver's license shows he moved to another state right afterward. Detective Chaplin does not believe the last piece of information in the prepared police report is even relevant to the present case. He is not surprised at the lack of relevant information due to the short time allowed to produce the report. Zeus also has no reason to expect Martin Goodwill to have a criminal record, so it would make sense that his police file would be thin or non-existent.

Myrtle, on the other hand, is quite the opposite of Zeus. Being a citizen, she is free to take liberties that the Detective cannot because she does not have to answer for her actions in the same way that he does. She sits in silence and ponders Goody's testimony before finally speaking. "Well Detective, he does have a history of addictive compulsive behavior. It is possible he was driven to violence when his attempts to satisfy his fetish urges were unsuccessful." Myrtle believes Goody exhibits traits of narcissism that could possibly lead him to behave badly to protect his ego. She believes he had a possible motive and he definitely had the opportunity. He could easily have acted while the lights were off. Goody is strong enough to create enough force to seriously injure Porsha.

CHAPTER 14

Zeus and Myrtle do not have time to comb over the fine details of the last interview right now, so they table the conversation. They have already spotted the second person on their list and are making their way toward her. The description Ms. Marmalade provided them was extremely accurate. Myrtle marvels at how easily Zeus cuts through the crowd, she wonders if this is a part of the police training? It is like he can anticipate where the person ahead of him is going to step and then he steps the other way. She trails him through the parted sea of people all the way to the manicured feet of their second suspect.

"Good morning ma'am, I'm Detective Chaplin, and this is Ms. Jenson."

Zeus once again discloses how Myrtle is assisting the police but is not a police officer. The second suspect's name is Roxanne Williams. She is aware of who Detective Chaplin is, she remembers him from the night before. The Detective asks her to state her full name for the record.

Myrtle notices how Zeus's tone appears kinder toward this suspect and wonders if it is because the dress Roxanne is wearing shows all of her curves. Then again, Goody was a bit of a jerk so maybe that affected Zeus's attitude toward him. Either way, Myrtle notices a difference and she does not like it. Although they are not dating, the thought of Zeus possibly looking at other women makes her jealous. Moments go by before Myrtle realizes that Roxanne is well into her first answer. She wonders how long she has been daydreaming about Zeus's tone? Myrtle is embarrassed by her lack of attention. Zeus does not seem to even notice that Myrtle was not mentally present. He waits for Roxanne to finish talking and continues with the next question.

"Ms. Williams, can you tell us what you remember about last night along with your whereabouts at the time of the murder?" Zeus may not have noticed Myrtle's distant look earlier but Roxanne certainly did. "You can call me Roxy. Is this interview going to take long?", she asks. Roxy points out that there is no point in her giving answers if nobody is listening to her. Zeus assures Roxy they are paying very close attention to what she is saying. "Ms. Williams, I know this is a long process, but it is possible what happened last night was not an accident," reasons Detective Chaplin. "If you could please, tell us what you remember about last night." Roxy feels a little better about giving her statement after being assured she has their attention. Plus, she reminds herself that Zeus is a police detective and she does not want to risk looking like she has something to hide. If the police believe she has something to do with the crime, it may lead to her being detained in Viewgrove or possibly jailed. With that in mind, she begins to explain what she remembers happening. "The lights went off, I got on my cell phone to check my timeline while I waited. After the lights came back on, I heard a scream so I looked over and there were people standing over by where, you know, Porsha was."

Myrtle carefully studies Roxy's body language for clues while she gives her statement to Detective Chaplin. People give off both verbal and non-verbal cues while talking. At times the non-verbal cues can be more revealing. It definitely feels like Roxy is trying to influence Detective Chaplin with her tantalizing tone. Myrtle wonders if the detective even notices the manipulation attempt. "He is a man", she thinks to herself, of course, he does not notice. Roxy's account of the events of the previous night sound very similar to what Goody told them. Myrtle injects herself into the interview.

"Did you know Porsha, the young lady that died?"

"Yes, I did, Porsha was my friend."

Roxy explains how she came to Viewgrove to support her friend. Porsha had mentioned how she was excited to be competing this week. She was already a pageant crown holder and Roxy could tell she was focused on winning this pageant as well. Some of the other contestants seemed to take this pageant less seriously and were just happy to have been selected.

Detective Chaplin asks a follow-up question, "Ms. Williams, Roxy, do you recall seeing Sheila and Porsha together last night?" Roxy looks confused, "Who is Sheila?" Before the Detective could answer she continues on, "I did see that pageant judge Goody talking to Porsha at least once last night, have you questioned him yet?" Myrtle asks Roxy if she is positive it was Goody and Porsha that she saw? "Oh, I'm positive, it was them," replies Roxy, "I couldn't hear what they were saying but it was definitely them." Roxy demands the police stop wasting time with her and go out and catch whoever did this to her friend. "We're doing our best ma'am," responds Detective Chaplin, "thank you for your time and cooperation."

Zeus and Myrtle say goodbye to Roxy and wander far enough to feel they are not within earshot of anybody before getting each other's reactions to the interview. "Well that was also interesting," begins Detective Chaplin, "I don't think she's a strong suspect, what do you think Myrtle?"

"I think her dress is too tight," quips Myrtle.

"Say what?" responds Zeus, confused by where that came from.

Myrtle does not even bother to address his confusion, "Detective, is there any additional information on the police background report regarding Ms. Williams?" Zeus begins to review the prepared report with her, "Her name is Roxanne Denise Williams." The county records list her as unmarried. Her driver's license is suspended but lists her age as thirty-seven, and height approximately 5 feet 5 inches tall. Her last employer is unknown. She does have several complaints filed against her for extortion, some as recently as late last year. It appears she has never spent any time in jail, none of the cases resulted in convictions. It looks like the plaintiffs always ended up dropping the charges. Detective Chaplin has a little more concern after reading the details in Roxy's police report. Just because there are no convictions on her record does not mean that something did not happen, it could be the plaintiff did not feel it was worth the trouble or it is possible they were coerced into dropping the charges. From the look on Myrtle's face, the Detective believes she could be thinking along the same lines regarding these complaints.

Once again, Myrtle does not say anything right away. She ponders Roxy's testimony along with the results from the background report in silence. "Well Detective, she does have a history of manipulation." Ms. Marmalade had expressed to them that Porsha was heavily favored to win the pageant. Is it possible Roxy needed Porsha to fix the pageant results for some reason or another and she refused? Myrtle believes Roxy exhibits a vital need to be in control, what could be considered as a need for power. She is not above extortion and manipulation. Roxy claims Porsha was her good friend but she could have invited herself on this trip. If they had a toxic relationship, then Roxy would need to stay close at all times to control her. Myrtle makes herself a note to ask Porsha's family if they know Roxy and if she traveled to all of the pageants that Porsha competed in. The two women also could have had a simple disagreement that ended tragically. Roxy could easily have slipped away while the lights were off; she had the opportunity. Roxy's possible motive is not clear at this time.

CHAPTER 15

Two suspects down and one to go. There were other interviews to be taken but these three were the main focus today. Zeus and Myrtle were making good progress today. The word has gotten out that the police are conducting interviews and their third interviewee finds them. Detective Chaplin turns around to greet their guest. "Good morning ma'am, my name is Detective Chaplin, and this is Ms. Jenson." As with the other two interviews, Zeus discloses that Myrtle Jenson is assisting the police in the investigation and is not an officer.

"My name is Sheila Johnson, I heard you were looking to speak to me."

Detective Chaplin welcomes Sheila into the interview, "Thank you for finding us, yes, we are looking to speak with you." Sheila enters the space and takes a seat. "You're welcome Detective," she replies, "How can I help?" Zeus Chaplin politely asks Sheila to tell them what she can remember regarding the night before. Myrtle keeps a watchful eye on Sheila's body language. She seemed upbeat and loose when she first walked in but now she appears to be tense. This change could either be an indication of deception or she could simply be uncomfortable with police questioning. "The police have already asked me everything they can think of, this is harassment!" snaps Sheila. Myrtle has no patience for this resistance and quickly responds before Zeus has a chance to. "Ms. Johnson, what happened last night was not an accident, we need your help to catch a possible murderer." Sheila is taken back by Myrtle being in her face and quickly decides she does not want any problems with her. Zeus puts his hands on Myrtle's shoulder to let her know she has gone too far. He is still in charge of the investigation and if anybody gets in somebody's face it will be him. Myrtle heeds Zeus's warning and quickly backs off. Sheila is thankful the Detective intervened.

"Oh, my Goodness, somehow I knew that?" sighs Sheila.

"Really, knew that how?" asks Zeus.

"I don't know, I just get a feeling about these things, just how she was lying there, something about it just didn't sit right with me," she replies. The Detective continues, "Ms. Johnson, we are aware of what happened to you at one of these events in the past." Sheila interrupts him, "Let me stop you right there before you even ask. Yes, I did have a psychotic episode but I take my medication faithfully and have not had one single episode since!" Sheila was not done, "If I were investigating this, I would check out Roxanne or Roxy or whatever her name is. My sister and I saw Roxy and Porsha having an argument backstage after one of the rehearsals. I do not even know why she is here since she is not even competing in the pageant. I hate that this happened to Porsha, my sister introduced me to her, she seemed like a nice person."

Tensions are running a little high in the room right now but Myrtle pushes on, "What do you know about Ms. Williams or Roxy?" Sheila pauses for a beat before answering, "I don't really know Roxy. She sat out in the audience as I did during one or two of the rehearsals. I only noticed her because she also seemed to have nothing to do with the show, like me, and the audience section was otherwise empty. Later on, my sister lets me know who Roxy was." She looked at Myrtle to see if she had any follow-up questions, and of course, she did. "So, nobody else came in that auditorium who wasn't in the pageant?" she questioned. Sheila insists nobody else came in because the rehearsals were closed and then she paused. "Wait, there was that judge, he stopped by a rehearsal for a minute. I didn't know he was a pageant judge back then." Myrtle, finally feeling like she is getting somewhere, presses, "Who, do you mean Mr. Goodwill?" Sheila confirms, "Yes, that's the one, Mr. Goodwill." Detective Chaplin warns Myrtle about suggesting names to Sheila and advises Sheila to be very sure before agreeing with any names suggested to her. Myrtle apologizes to both Sheila and the Detective and respectfully requests to ask one more question. "One last question Ms. Johnson, did you notice a cell phone by the victim's body that night?" "No, I didn't" replies Sheila. "Thank you for your time, ma'am." Detective Chaplin ends the interview and releases Sheila

Johnson back to the rest of the pageant population. "If you think of anything else please don't hesitate to contact us," concludes the Detective.

Zeus and Myrtle hustle off to excuse themselves once again to a private area of the Sunset Auditorium. "Well, what can I say, this is not getting any easier" begins Detective Chaplin, "I know I keep saying this but I can't rule her out as a suspect either." Myrtle nods her head in agreement. She asks how he knew about the previous psychotic episode. That one was easy, he had read part of the background research report while Sheila was making her way in. "Zeus, is there any additional information in the police report regarding Ms. Johnson?" He begins to review the remainder of the report. According to the report, her name is Sheila Marie Johnson. The county records list her as unmarried. Her driver's license lists her age as thirty-four, and height approximately 5 feet 7 inches tall. Sheila works as a real estate agent for a large real estate firm. She has an assault charge on her record from an incident two years ago. I do not know if the pageant organizers were aware of this but Sheila Johnson was a contestant in this very pageant only two years earlier. We know because there was a Police report filed. It appears during one of the early pageant meetings; she had a psychotic episode and attacked one of the other contestants. The pageant notified the police and they made the arrest. She did not serve any jail time but was admitted to a psychiatric ward for treatment. Subsequently, the pageant director dismissed her from the pageant. It appears that since then she has turned her life around and become a model citizen, no further arrests appear on her record. So, it appears she was telling the truth about her medication working. Zeus does not know how to feel about what he has just read in the report. He finds himself being suspicious of the fact she has returned to the pageant after what happened the last time, why would she do that? He puts himself in that situation and he cannot see returning to any pageant, let alone one where he committed an assault. He looks over to try and gauge where Myrtle's mind is at, she can be hard to read sometimes.

Myrtle stands, stone-faced, deep in thought. She ponders Sheila's testimony along with the results from the background report. She starts to talk but stops before she begins again, it was as if she changed her mind on how she wanted to phrase what she was about to say. "Well Detective, she does have a history of violence." Myrtle believes Sheila exhibits strong attachment traits. Sheila and her sister are very close. They grew especially close after Sheila's incident at this very pageant two years ago. The sister may have been one of Sheila's primary caregivers during her recovery. If for some reason Sheila perceived the highly favored Porsha as a threat to her sister's chances of winning the pageant, she could have attacked her to protect her sister. It is also possible that being back in this environment triggered another psychotic episode or flashback that caused her to act violently as well. Myrtle believes Sheila could easily have acted while the lights were off; she has both possible motive and opportunity. She could have confronted Porsha in the stairwell and pushed her to her death.

CHAPTER 16

Zeus and Myrtle take a moment to evaluate their progress in the investigation. There is a lot of information to process. Three interviews completed and zero suspects eliminated. Zeus and Myrtle may have their suspicions but they cannot absolutely rule out any of the interviewees based on what they have heard. This was definitely not the result they set out to achieve when they began. After the police interview, Goody makes his way to a vacant auditorium seat. He takes a seat to wait for the police to release everybody. This waiting is the worst, it is hard for him to recall a time when he has ever wanted to leave a place more. As he sits in the auditorium chair, quietly in his thoughts, he becomes aware of another presence. Without turning his head, he glances out of the corner of his eye to see who it is. At some time, unknown to him, Myrtle has also made her way to the auditorium and is occupying the seat over from him. Goody is now feeling very self-conscious and he wonders how long has she been there? Myrtle is aware that Goody has noticed her.

"I hope you don't mind me resting here Mr. Goodwill."

"I've been up since early this morning," she states.

"It's a free country," replies Goody.

"Please call me Goody, calling me Mr. Goodwill makes me feel like I'm in a courtroom." Myrtle turns in her seat to face Goody. "That's an odd reference, have you spent a lot of time in front of judges?" The look on Goody's face clearly lets her know this line of questioning is a dead-end. If looks could kill Myrtle would be dead where she sat. So, Myrtle adjusts her approach slightly in hopes of getting Goody to open up a bit. "Very well, Mr. Goodwill, I mean Goody, do you know anybody that would want to harm Porsha?"

Goody leans in toward Myrtle and lowers his voice as if he is sharing a secret. "You didn't hear it from me but if I were you, lady, I would have the police talk to that woman named Sheila. From what I could tell, Sheila and Porsha did not get along. Now that I think about it, I saw them arguing about something last night." Myrtle feels Goody is being a little reckless with his comments and wonders if any of this will be able to be proven. Sheila does have that history of violence so what Goody claims cannot be totally dismissed. What happened to that girl last night was very unfortunate, if what Goody says is true then she needs to investigate what he is saying. "Were you at all of the rehearsals, Mr. Goodwill, I mean Goody?" asks Myrtle. Goody glances to either side of him to make sure nobody else has sat down beside him without him noticing. The last thing he wants is for the Detective to be also sitting beside him without his knowledge. "No ma'am, I stopped by one rehearsal briefly about a week ago to talk to Ms. Marmalade", answers Goody. He is getting concerned that Myrtle may be twisting his words. Normally he would have blown her off, but if she is working with the police then he needs to be sure she tells his story correctly. He would hate to be accused simply because this nosy lady cannot keep the facts straight. Once he is sure Myrtle is paying close attention, he continues with the rest of his statement. "I stopped by briefly last night only to let Ms. Marmalade know I had lost my judges packet. I needed to know what time I should be here for the show, but I didn't stay long either time." Myrtle pushes a bit further and asks what he knows about Sheila. "Not much other than what I've already told you," answers Goody, "I believe her sister may be a current contestant in the pageant or something. Can I ask why you were asking about Porsha's cell phone?" Myrtle explains how she feels that finding the cell phone will lead the Police to the killer and close this case. "Thank you for your help Goody, I'll be sure to pass along the information you've provided to the police." Myrtle excuses herself and leaves him to be alone with his thoughts. Goody breathes a sigh of relief. He does not wish to show it but he is glad to see her leave.

Once again Goody becomes aware of another presence. "You're back already," he says without even looking up. "Back already? I think you have me confused with somebody else," the person answers. "Oh, it's you Ms. Marmalade," he says, "I thought you were that Jenson lady back again with more questions." Ms. Marmalade chuckles, "No, it's just me, I'm just waiting for them to release everybody. How are you holding up with everything, are you doing okay?" Goody nods his head slowly. "I'll be doing a lot better when I'm out of this small town and back at home." Ms. Marmalade tries to encourage him. "Hang in there, this will be over before you know it. What I came to tell you is the officer told me you're free to leave the auditorium but you can't leave town just yet." Just like that Ms. Marmalade is gone, almost as suddenly as she arrived. Goody is left to think about what she said. He decides Ms. Marmalade is correct and this will all be over before he knows it, he just has to hang in there. Having to answer Police questions is stressful. He feels like he did the best he could. Goody can only hope his answers came across the way he intended them to.

CHAPTER 17

Sheila walks out of her interview with Zeus and Myrtle visibly rattled. She wanders off to a vacant area of the Sunset Auditorium to regain her composure and collect her thoughts. As she starts to come back into herself, she gets the strange feeling she is not alone. Sheila turns and peers straight behind her into the dimly lit parts of the theater but does not see anyone. This old theater creeps her out. Her mind flashes to every horror movie she has ever seen where creatures hide in the dark waiting to prey on unsuspecting campers or cheerleaders. She tries to shake it off and tells herself it is all in her mind but she cannot shake the feeling of being watched. Sheila's instincts are correct. Unknown to her, an unseen visitor starts to emerge from the shadows out of her view. With each passing moment, the visitor moves closer and closer until they share the same space. "Would you like an aspirin Ms. Johnson?" asks Myrtle from seemingly nowhere. "Ahh, you scared me!" exclaims Sheila while clutching her chest. To answer your question, "No aspirin, but I really just need to sit down for a minute, and I could use a drink after that scare."

"I'm sorry for scaring you Ms. Johnson," apologizes Myrtle. As she approached she could see Sheila but Sheila could not see her. In that moment she realized how easy it would be to attack somebody from the shadows. Myrtle wonders how well Sheila knows her way around the auditorium. "Oh wow, I see why you jumped," says Myrtle staring back at the darkness she just emerged from. "You could really jump out and surprise somebody." Myrtle watches Sheila's body language carefully for any reaction to her comment but there is none. Sheila does not appear to know anything about any shadow attacks so Myrtle moves ahead with her next question.

"Can you tell me, what is your connection to the pageant?"

Sheila tends to ramble a bit when she is nervous, and Myrtle makes her nervous. She explains that her younger sister is a current contestant in the pageant. She has recently reunited with her sister. They have the same father but different mothers so they grew up in different homes. Sheila is at the pageant solely to support her sister. She has taken time off from work to travel there. She and her sister are bonding while sharing a hotel room. Sheila has never been to Viewgrove before, the town seems a little too slow for her liking, she is used to the big city life. She has always been the more outgoing of the two sisters. Sheila was a contestant in the Ms. Plus-No Fuss Pageant three years ago. Her younger sister was inspired to participate in the pageant this year based on her sister's experience three years ago. It was a chance for her to gain some self-confidence and personal growth through the pageant activities. Unfortunately, she was not able to complete her goal of competing in the pageant. During a pause in the conversation, Sheila admits to Myrtle that she is a little worried about the Pageant Director recognizing her. Sheila looks very different than she did at the time she participated in the pageant. Her hair is a different color and in a different style. She dresses differently and carries herself in a very different way. Also, at that time, she went by her middle name.

Myrtle understands that Sheila guards her secret closely, she has left that old life behind, and it is not something she wants people in her new life to know about. She wonders what lengths Sheila would go to protect her new life. "Since we're being honest," begins Sheila, "My sister warned me to stay out of Roxy's way, she called her crazy." Sheila apologizes to Myrtle for not mentioning it during the initial interview with Detective Chaplin. She appears to retreat into her thoughts so Myrtle figures that is the most she is going to get out of her today. With that in mind, she says goodbye. "Do you know how much longer we have to stay here?" asks Sheila before Myrtle is out of earshot. Myrtle stops long enough to answer, "It shouldn't be too much longer." Sheila looks up in time to see Ms. Marmalade heading toward her. She watches as Myrtle and Ms. Marmalade pass by each other and exchange fake pleasantries. Sheila finds their exchange kind of funny, and she knows a forced greeting when she sees one. The moment brings her a short feeling of joy in what has otherwise been a stressful day.

Ms. Marmalade is now close enough to speak, "How are you doing honey, are you holding up okay? I'm just checking on everybody." Sheila forces a smile, "I'm okay, I'm just hoping this whole thing is over soon." Ms. Marmalade pulls her in for a tight hug. "Me too." As she pulls back from the embrace she looks at Sheila for a moment, "You look a little familiar, have we met before?" Before Sheila can even answer, somebody calls Ms. Marmalade's name and she turns to head toward them. "I'll be back to check on you a little later. If you need anything let me or somebody on the staff know." As she leaves she advises there is lots of water on hand, and she will order food if they are kept there much longer. Sheila breathes a sigh of relief that Ms. Marmalade is called away, that was just in time. She makes a note to herself to be sure to avoid her going forward, that was too close for comfort. As soon as Ms. Marmalade walks away, an officer walks up to inform Sheila she is free to go back to her hotel but may be called upon later. She thanks the officer and heads for the front door. Sheila does not care about leaving town, she is just glad to be getting out of that auditorium. At least at the hotel, she can order room service and relax in the hot tub. In the auditorium, there is nothing to do but wait and gossip about who did it. It feels like a bad episode of one of those shows where a group of strangers is locked in the house with little communication with the outside world.

CHAPTER 18

Roxy is at the water cooler getting a drink to calm her nerves when none other than Myrtle approaches her. Roxy had noticed her talking to Goody and Sheila but was hoping she did not make her way around to her. She is just not in the mood for more questions right now. Yet, here she is, about to invade her space. Myrtle appears harmless enough but Roxy believes it is all an act. She believes Myrtle is a lot savvier than she would have people believe. "Is the water cold?" inquires Myrtle as she steps out of the shadows and into view. She studies Roxy's body language closely for any clues. Roxy does not appear either startled or confused by Myrtle's emergence from the darkness. "It's cold," Roxy answers calmly, "Please, help yourself." She tries to step away but Myrtle follows her. "Do you mind if we talk while I drink?" Myrtle asks in her most pleasant voice. Roxy grudgingly makes the decision to talk to her, maybe if she answers a few questions Myrtle will move on to the next person. Her fear is if she does not talk to her now Myrtle will keep finding excuses to come and talk to her later. Roxy forces a toothless smile before answering, "Sure, what would you like to talk about?" Myrtle smiles back and once again in her most pleasant voice asks her question. "During the Police interview, you told the Detective you saw Porsha talking to Mr. Goodwill. What do you know about Mr. Goodwill?" Roxy's face crunches up like she is trying to figure out who Myrtle is talking about. "I believe you may know him as Goody," offers Myrtle in an attempt to clear the confusion. "Oh, Goody, only the gossip I've heard," answers Roxy. She goes on to explain how she heard Goody loves to pick up women in bars, with the pick-up line, Goody got it! Roxy cannot even say it without laughing, "Come on, who says that?" She heard he is a rising star at one of the biggest accounting firms in the country. Roxy feels comfortable saying whatever is on her mind with no regard for Myrtle or anybody else for that matter. She reveals how she thought she recognized Goody sitting in the rehearsal a week ago. His face looked familiar but initially, she could not think where she knew him from. Then it hit her, is that the guy with the plus-size fetish? She would have to confirm it with her friend Porsha after rehearsal, but she is sure that is him. She has a sick feeling in her stomach because Porsha had a short fling with Goody in the past that did not end well.

"Do you know anything about Sheila Johnson?" asks Myrtle. She described Sheila to Roxy. "Oh no, I don't really know her, I just saw her around the pageant with one of the contestants." Myrtles nods along just to show she is listening and paying attention. She does not want a reoccurrence of the last time they spoke. Her intent is for this to feel like a casual conversation, not a police interrogation. Perhaps a lighter question is what is in order. "How did you become involved with the pageant?" asks Myrtle. Roxy shares some of her story, "I learned about this pageant from my friend Porsha, she competes in pageants all of the time." Roxy traveled down to Viewgrove to support Porsha and get some girlfriend bonding time in. Porsha had originally planned to rent a car and come by herself until Roxy agreed to drive down with her. That was a week ago. Roxy had some unused vacation time so she did not mind. They were able to split the cost of the hotel and the travel which was a big help to Porsha. "May I ask you a question, did you notice a cell phone by Porsha's body that night?" Roxy shakes her head, "No, I didn't, I was in too much shock to notice anything." Myrtle nods her head in acknowledgment and thanks her for all of her help. Roxy strikes Myrtle as a very direct person, somebody who tells you exactly how they feel. So why does she get the feeling Roxy is leaving something out? Roxy has never claimed to be an angel and whatever secret she is guarding could spell trouble for her if ever revealed. Myrtle departs, leaving Roxy to enjoy her water.

Just then a familiar face arrives. "Old lady Myrtle didn't look that thirsty to me!", quips the boisterous Ms. Marmalade. Roxy could not help but laugh because she was thinking the same thing when Myrtle approached her. "You looked like you needed a laugh honey, she's a real nosy lady, isn't she?" states Ms. Marmalade. "Yes, she is," answers Roxy, "and yes, I did need a laugh, so thank you." Ms. Marmalade cracks a half smile, "I'm sure she'll be looking for me next, so I can't sit still for too long." She questions if Myrtle can even ask them questions because she is not a police officer. "That nosy lady needs to mind her business and leave the rest of us alone, let the police do their work." Ms. Marmalade encourages Roxy to hang in there, they are starting to let people go. "Let me go before she circles back with more questions," laughs Ms. Marmalade as she gets up and heads off. Sheila happens to pass Roxy on her way out of the auditorium. "Oh, can we leave?" asks Roxy. "They are releasing people, you should check and see if you're free to leave," replies Sheila. Roxy hurries off to find an officer to request permission to leave the auditorium, she cannot wait to get out of there. She wonders around for a few minutes looking for an officer to confirm what Sheila has told her. Now that she needs an officer she is unable to find one. She cannot wait to get out of not only the auditorium, but the hotel, and the whole town. If she never sees these people again it will be too soon.

CHAPTER 19

"This wait is killing me," complains Ms. Marmalade before she realizes what a poor choice of words that is. She looks around to see if anybody heard that. Nobody appears to be paying any attention to her. Ms. Marmalade's frustration comes from the speed of the investigation. The Police have not released the Sunset Auditorium from being a crime scene so the pageant is unable to proceed with the show. The tickets have been sold, the advertising has already been paid for, and the cost of renting the venue is non-refundable. The Ms. Plus-No Fuss pageant is in danger of losing a great deal of money if the show has to be postponed or canceled. Ms. Marmalade is feeling the pressure of the show date fast approaching and is pressuring the police department to close the case or risk facing legal action. At the very least allow them to use the auditorium for the show, a new venue would be difficult to secure at this late a date.

Ms. Marmalade decides she needs to try and

minimize her financial losses. She starts to prepare a legal argument for why she was entitled to a refund of a portion of the venue fees. Her plan is to argue that the local police mishandled the investigation and caused delays that were out of her control. The police department is also facing pressure from the Sunset Auditorium itself. The Sunset Auditorium Board is embarrassed their building is associated with a crime scene and would like the whole ugly incident resolved immediately. If people start to associate the auditorium with a crime it will decrease the number of bookings and discourage patrons from attending events there. There is a lot of tension among all parties involved. Detective Zeus Chaplin understands the other parties' position, he knows there could be damage to the town's tourism economy. However, Zeus also believes in his obligation to uncover the truth if a crime has been committed. Myrtle meets back up with Zeus and attempts to act as natural as possible. Zeus has no idea she has been off talking to suspects without him.

"Where have you been Myrtle?"

"Oh nowhere, Detective, just went to get a drink of water," she answers.

Just then a frustrated Ms. Marmalade storms up to Zeus and Myrtle yelling and waving a cell phone in their faces. "What are we supposed to be looking at ma'am?" calmly asks the Detective. "These are receipts, oh wait, there are a bunch of fingerprint smudges on my screen," Ms. Marmalade pulls the phones down and wipes the screen clean. "Okay, look now," she waves the phone back in their faces, "This is all of the money I'm going to lose if the show doesn't go on as scheduled!" Detective Chaplin calms Ms. Marmalade down by kindly reminding her that threatening an officer is a criminal offense. At that moment it hits Myrtle, "That's it!" She quickly hatches a plan and discusses it with Detective Chaplin who reluctantly agrees. Zeus agrees to support Myrtle's plan mainly because he does not have a better idea at this point, and his department is under a lot of pressure. Everybody wants this case wrapped up yesterday. Zeus knows he cannot keep interviewing these people without probable cause and will most likely have to close the case without an arrest. It is clear the pageant participants are tired of being questioned and may begin to request lawyers if they have not already. There has not been any new evidence or clues uncovered. The crime department could be subject to a lot of scrutiny for the way this case was handled, especially if there is no arrest or conviction. With all of this weighing on his mind, he calls up Officer Leighton at the police station and sets Myrtle's plan in motion.

Officer Leighton arrives at the Sunset Auditorium and searches for Myrtle and Zeus. He locates them at the corner of the stage discussing the case. The young officer is reluctant to interrupt them because it looks like whatever they are discussing is very important. He tries to wait a few moments for a pause in their conversation. Maybe they will notice him and give him their attention. However, there does not seem to be a lull in their conversation so he may end up standing there for a while. "Excuse me Detective" he interrupts. "Yes Officer," replies Zeus, "What is it?" Officer Leighton straightens up. "Sorry to interrupt sir," he begins, "I just thought you may want to know somebody called in an anonymous tip on the case.

The caller disguised his or her voice." Finally, a possible lead in the case. Myrtle and Zeus listen intently, both are hanging on the officer's every word. "Well, what did the tipster say," interrupts an impatient Zeus Chaplin. "Sorry Detective," apologizes Officer Leighton, "The tipster insisted if we search the personal belongings of the people still present in the auditorium we will find the victim's missing cell phone." Detective Chaplin questions the young officer again, "Are you sure that is all that was said?". Officer Leighton confirms again that this was the entire message. Detective Chaplin releases the young officer to his other duties and then turns his attention toward Myrtle. Zeus motions for them to move to a secluded corner where they are unlikely to be overheard by anybody else in the building. They make their way to the chosen area while making sure they are not being followed. "Okay Myrtle, the tipster part of your plan went smooth, so what's the next step?" Myrtle met his gaze with a confused look on her face.

"The thing is Detective, I didn't arrange that tipster call, that wasn't part of my plan."

"Wait, what?", exclaims the Detective, "You mean that was a real tip?"

CHAPTER 20

Detective Chaplin is beginning to believe he may have made a mistake by agreeing to execute Myrtle's proposal. It is early in the process and things are already not going according to plan. Myrtle can sense the change in Zeus's demeanor, and can only imagine what he must be thinking. The tipster phone call really has the Detective's mind churning. Myrtle found the call from the anonymous tipster more puzzling than exciting. Both Zeus and Myrtle were desperate for new clues but a tipster is a variable she had not accounted for. She wonders who this tipster is and how do they know what they know? Myrtle found it curious the tipster mentioned the victim's missing cell phone, that was not a detail mentioned in any news coverage she had seen. She does her best to convince Zeus they can still use this new development to their advantage. "I know how we can still make this work in our favor." The look on Zeus's face says he is not so sure. So Myrtle makes her argument for how they can use the new information to help solve the case.

"I hear you, but I just don't know?" replies Detective Chaplin.

"Do you think it will work? I hope it does because it won't be easy to actually get a warrant to search all of these personal belongings without probable cause." After some prodding, Zeus comes around to Myrtle's way of thinking and agrees to trust her plan. It is not like he has a better option at the moment or a plan of his own. Besides, he trusts Myrtle's instincts. He has witnessed her be right so many times in those court cases that she has earned the benefit of the doubt. Myrtle is not oblivious to the trust the Detective is putting in her. She realizes the tough position Zeus is in and is determined not to let him down. They both know that there is a lot at stake here. If this investigation goes wrong there will be a lot of explaining to do and that could result in some demotions or even worse, terminations. "Well Detective," begins Myrtle, "We just give it a moment to circulate that the Police will be searching everybody's belongings for the cell phone and see what kind of response we get." Myrtle is betting if this plays right there will be no need to try and get warrants or probable cause. They both discreetly move into position, while trying to act as normal as possible. They send word to the hotel where the participants are staying about a search rumor. Time is of the essence, something has to be done to change the course of the investigation. Sometimes when under pressure, the perpetrators may tip their hand and make a mistake that leads to their capture. Detective Chaplin and Myrtle are hoping for something to break this case wide open. They both camp out on the catwalk above the stage, close to some stage lights and out of sight. From this vantage point, they can secretly watch everybody in the theater. The Sunset Auditorium is empty as the occupants have been released. Zeus and Myrtle are curious to observe if anybody acts on the rumor they have spread at the hotel.

The Detective is most interested in the three non-contestants, Sheila, Goody, and Roxy. He has a hunch they hold the key to solving the case in some way. Is it possible the three of them know each other outside of just meeting at the pageant? Trying to be as quiet as possible, Zeus leans in to ask a question. "Why did you ask the Pageant Director about a cell phone?" Myrtle answers him without moving or taking her eyes off the stage below, "Young people feel lost without their phones, if we can locate it, it could provide a clue to what Porsha was doing in her final moments." Myrtle has a question for him. "Were you able to get the judge to approve the search warrants for the hotel rooms of the people in the pageant like we discussed?" Zeus answers in a low whisper, "I sent the request, it wasn't easy, I had to call in a special favor." Myrtle feels confident everything is in place. "Please make sure your officers follow my specific instructions," she answers.

The Sunset Auditorium catwalk is the perfect place to people watch. Zeus Chaplin does not know what he honestly expects to see but he trusts Myrtle's instincts and she insists they observe the theater for a little while. He decides to treat it the same way he would a police stakeout. It is a waiting game at this point. "How can you see anything from up here, I thought you wore glasses?" whispers the Detective. "I wear reading glasses, I can see things from this distance just fine", she assures him. Zeus can feel her hazel eyes burning a hole in his neck but he does not turn his eyes to meet hers. He is happy to wait as long as it takes for this moment to pass. Plus, this stakeout gives him an opportunity to spend time with her. Myrtle has a hunch and there are three people, in particular, she is keeping an extra eye out for. Everything seems to be normal and it feels like they have been waiting for hours. Just at the point where she is starting to second guess this whole idea she observes something. If Myrtle had blinked too long she would have missed it. From the catwalk above, she observes somebody move quickly across the stage. She wonders if she saw what she thinks she saw and tries to confirm it with the Detective. "Over there Detective, did you see that?" Zeus looks toward where she is pointing. "See what?" The Detective springs back to life and is on alert now. They both watch as the mystery person re-emerges and stashes a concealed object under the side stairwell. The shadowy figure disappears out of the auditorium, but not before Zeus and Myrtle both get a good look at her face.

"Come on Zeus, we're going down there. Gather your officers, we need to find what is under that stairwell." Zeus and Myrtle emerge from their hiding spot and make their way down toward the stairwell.

CHAPTER 21

"Let's be thorough officers, make sure you check this whole area, including the spots you checked yesterday," orders Zeus Chaplin. Myrtle and Zeus look on intently as the police officers perform a search of the area. Officer Leighton approaches Zeus with a confused look on his face. "Sir", he begins and then continues without waiting for a response, "We already searched this area yesterday and came up with nothing." Everybody involved with this case is frustrated and feeling the pressure. "I know my fellow officers, and I am satisfied that they conducted a thorough sweep of the area yesterday," states the young officer. "Perhaps you could tell me what prompted this additional search?" Myrtle pretends not to hear the officer's question and completely ignores him, she is focused intently on the officers searching the left stage area. Detective Chaplin turns his attention away from the search to address Officer Leighton's concern. "Officer", he growls, "We are trying to solve a murder case here, and if it requires we search this whole auditorium ten more

times then that's what we'll do, is that understood?"
Officer Leighton falls back into line. "Understood sir, I'll
rejoin the search immediately." Leighton is a promising
officer who hopes to make detective one day. It is not his
intent to second guess the lead detective or get on his bad
side, he looks up to Zeus too much for that. He resigns
himself to the idea that if Detective Chaplin wants them to
search this area again then he must have a good reason.
Myrtle turns her head slightly toward Detective Chaplin,
"police drama Detective?" Zeus denies that there is any
drama. "No drama Myrtle", he replies, "Leighton is a good
officer, he just needs to learn some patience, this is the
most action he's seen in three months so he's just a little
excitable right now."

"Detective, we found it, right around where you
thought it would be," announces a triumphant police
officer. "Thank you, Officer Leighton, please bag and tag
it," instructs Zeus Chaplin. Zeus examines the cell phone
once it is in the evidence bag. To his amazement the
device still has life, the clock still has the correct time. The
phone survived the impact of hitting the floor and the
battery still held a charge. The Detective is not familiar
with smartphones, he knows how to work his flip phone
but that is about it. In Zeus's world phones are strictly for
talking on. He is anxious to check the phone's memory
and call history but for now, he hands it back to the officer
to be taken back for processing. Officer Leighton offers to
check the call history on the phone. He is about to scroll
through the phone when Detective Chaplin yells.

"Wait, don't turn it on, that's evidence!"

"There could be some prints on there, let the guys in the lab process it first!"

The embarrassed officer lowers the phone. Zeus Chaplin has a better idea. "Officer, did Ms. Marmalade provide the victim's phone number?" The request sends young Leighton scrolling through his tablet where he finds it. "Good, you found it, would you please dial it," requests the Detective. The officer pulls out his smartphone and dials the cell phone number. The reception inside the Sunset Auditorium is spotty at best but the call goes through and sure enough, the phone in the evidence bag begins to light up and vibrate. This is definitely Porsha's phone. "Is there any update regarding the hotel search warrants?" inquires Zeus. "No sir, I'll request an update right away," responds Officer Leighton as he gets back on his phone to request an update. The young officer is not sure why they are trying to get a search warrant but he does not want to risk questioning the Detective again, it did not go so well the last time. He will do as he is told but he is not very confident they will actually receive what they are requesting. Officer Leighton is motivated to get the warrants, he does not want to disappoint the Detective again. Officer Leighton considers Detective Chaplin his mentor although he has never disclosed this to him. He has researched Zeus's career and learned about his career path. The Officer's hope is following a similar path will lead him to also have a distinguished career. One day Officer Leighton hopes to be able to tell the Detective what an inspiration he is to him but in the meantime, he prefers to be inspired from a distance.

CHAPTER 22

On Myrtle's request, Detective Chaplin summons the pageant participants back to the Sunset Auditorium. Once they arrive at the auditorium, wrangling everybody to the stage takes a few minutes. Even though the crime scene has been cleaned up and the caution tape has been removed people instinctively stay clear of it. Pageant participants are still dealing with the trauma and do not want to be anywhere near the crime scene. The few stragglers finally follow Detective Chaplin's instruction and at last everyone is gathered at the stage. Zeus blows his police whistle to quiet the grumbling crowd so Myrtle can address them. The pageant participants are fed up with all of these gatherings and questions. Some pageant contestants are even considering withdrawing. They hope they are being gathered for the last time to announce the investigation is closed. Myrtle explains to everyone that they have been gathered to re-enact the events of the night of the murder, only this time with the lights on.

Myrtle has everyone stand where they were that night. The contestants are not eager to perform a reenactment. They have been detained, questioned, and now this. Myrtle's request is mostly met with groans of protest and little actual movement. It is Ms. Marmalade who encourages the contestants to participate in the activity. These are the contestants she recruited and they are looking to her to confirm this is all okay.

"It's okay everybody, let's just do as this elderly woman asks. The sooner this investigation is over the sooner we can return to some semblance of normal."

Myrtle starts to respond to Ms. Marmalade's "elderly woman" comment but decides against it. It is killing her not to respond, but her goal is to get cooperation so she will hold her tongue, this time. Ms. Marmalade also complies and takes her position off stage. The pageant contestants take their places on the stage. Myrtle takes Porsha's place. Sheila, Roxy, and Goody take their places in the audience. It is all very unsettling to most to have to re-live that moment. With the suspects and Detective Chaplin all present on the auditorium stage, Myrtle delivers her theory on who killed Porsha. "What if I told you the person who dealt the deadly blow to Porsha is standing among us right now?" All eyes focused on Myrtle. "I'd have to say you were guessing," calls out Roxy. Myrtle ignores Roxy's outburst and continues to explain herself to the shocked faces in the auditorium. "Everything is as it was that night. At some point, the lights go out and the killer makes his or her move." Myrtle now assumes the role of the killer. She explains how the killer uses the darkness to his or her advantage to maneuver to the side of the stage. She believes the fact that the lighting went out that night was just an added bonus. "The light by the side stairs was out which means the killer had set a trap, and therefore what happened to Porsha was not an accident. The killer only intended it to look like an accident. The victim's body showed no evidence of any weapon used."

"What makes you say that?", interrupts Sheila.

"The medical examiner report shows no evidence of bullet wounds, knife stabbings, or poisoning," answers Myrtle before returning to her reenactment. "While everyone is preoccupied with the rehearsal, the killer waits for Porsha to be alone by the stairs and ambushes her. I found it quite easy to hide in the shadows of this theater." The audience listens intently as Myrtle demonstrates how the killer then blends back in with the people in the auditorium to wait for the body to be discovered. "The perpetrator's getaway is made easier by the house lights being down, his or her movement is harder to detect in the shadows. Once Porsha's body is discovered, the killer mingles with the crowd and pretends to be as shocked as everybody else. We are all gathered here today because we have identified the killer and it is time to make an arrest." Ms. Marmalade is the first one to speak out, "Now wait a minute! Everybody knows Porsha's death was a total accident, do you even have proof it wasn't? We can't start the healing process when the Police keep making these wild accusations!"

CHAPTER 23

A few murmurs can be heard from the crowd. "Why did you even ask us to come back here?" questions Roxy in an aggressive tone. "I can answer that for you," steps in Zeus Chaplin. "We gathered everyone here because we found it." The crowd looks very puzzled. "You found what?" asks Sheila. "We found the cell phone you tried to hide under the stairwell, Porsha's phone," replies Zeus. Sheila protests and is insulted by the accusation. After all, anybody could have put that phone there. "We observed you from the catwalk Sheila, you were seen trying to dispose of evidence," replies the Detective. He explains he has a strong hunch that when the cell phone is dusted for fingerprints they will find Sheila's prints all over it. "Sheila Johnson, you are under arrest for the murder of Porsha Jones! Officer, please arrest Ms. Johnson and advise her of her Miranda rights."

"Wait, I found that cell phone stuffed in the back of my locker backstage, I didn't take it, I found it in my sweater pocket" cries Sheila, as she is being handcuffed and read her rights. Sheila can hardly believe what is happening to her, it all feels like a bad dream. Her life was flashing before her eyes. She scanned the room frantically for somebody, anybody to help her. The week started off with her traveling to a pageant to support her sister and now she was being accused of murder. It was too much for her to process. She could hardly get out her next sentences. "I went to get my sweater yesterday and there it was, I don't know how it got there." She admits she figured it probably belonged to the victim and she panicked. If she came forward with the phone she knew the police would think she had something to do with what happened. Once she heard about the Police search, Sheila believed her only choice was to get rid of the phone and make it look like it slid under the stairs after the accident. Sheila's sister had to be held back by police officers as she attempted to rush to her sister's aid. The two sisters became hysterical in protest of Sheila's innocence. Sheila continued to cry out, "You have to believe me. You're making a big mistake Detective!"

From where Zeus is standing, it looks like Sheila is the one who made a big mistake. She would not be the first police suspect to proclaim their innocence. Despite her protests, she just became the police department's prime suspect. Perhaps she and Porsha got into some sort of argument that night that got out of control and Sheila pushed her down the stairs in anger. Stranger things have happened. Some of the people interviewed have stated they witnessed the two of them arguing at times. Perhaps Sheila had another episode and considered Porsha the biggest threat to her sister's chances of winning the pageant so she took action to get rid of her. Sheila's past sets a precedence for her violent behavior. Zeus makes a note to himself to have a trained specialist evaluate Sheila's state of mind to determine if there is any evidence of a breakdown. As for the cell phone, criminals have been known to keep mementos from their victims. Zeus believes Sheila probably kept the phone to delete any information she might have had in there about her and then tried to place it back at the crime scene when she became aware the police were looking for it. Zeus advises Sheila she can give her full statement at the police station. Some of the contestants have gathered around Sheila's sister to support her and keep her calm. Another outburst from her and possibly both sisters would be heading down to the police station. An excited Officer Leighton approaches both Zeus and Myrtle. He pulls them both aside to share the outcome of the hotel search warrants. Detective Chaplin and Myrtle hang on every word with anticipation. Officer Leighton begins to dive into the whole process that led up to the outcome. Zeus Chaplin finally interrupts and instructs the young officer to cut through the details and get straight to the point.

"The warrants were approved and they found it", Officer Leighton blurts out.

"They found it!", echoes Myrtle.

Officer Leighton is disappointed he did not get to explain all of the hard work that went into the process. He confirms the update from the officers at the hotel and then excuses himself to look for another officer that will care about his story.

CHAPTER 24

"Wait just a minute Detective," breaks in Myrtle, "Sheila may not be a fan of Porsha, but she is not our killer!" It is clear to her that the killer just wants them to think Sheila is the killer. "Are Sheila's fingerprints all over the recovered cell phone?", possibly, she submits. "The phone has to be processed but I am sure that they are," replies Zeus. "So, ask yourself, Detective, if she was the killer, wouldn't she have wiped her prints from the phone before returning it to the crime scene?" Zeus Chaplin does not have a quick comeback for that question.

Myrtle makes her case, "The killer took advantage of the lighting failure to commit the murder under the cover of darkness. The same killer also broke back into the Sunset Auditorium later that night. I know because I interrupted him or her when I circled back to look at the crime scene. The killer even went as far as to attack me. For the longest time, I could not think what the killer was doing that night, what they had come back for?" She shares how she remembers lying on the floor on the night of the attack and staring at the ceiling light fixture, trying to make sense of it. "It didn't hit me until I saw Ms. Marmalade struggling to rub her fingerprints off of her smartphone screen. She was waving it in the Detective's face while going on about the money she was going to lose. At some time during the rehearsal, while everybody was concentrating on what was happening on stage, the killer unscrewed the light bulb in the side stage stairwell to keep it from coming on so it would remain dark in that area. After the police arrived, the killer must have heard me remark to them how the Sunset Auditorium had recently completed testing of all of the lighting systems. He or she must have concluded it would be odd if a bulb was unscrewed where the crime was committed. The culprit planned to return to the auditorium that night to screw the light bulb back in. Once the police announced they were going to continue with the investigation, the killer needed a better plan. How would they explain their prints being discovered on the light bulb? It is not easy to wipe a light bulb clean of just your prints. A light bulb with absolutely no prints would also raise suspicion. It makes more sense to simply replace the bulb. Not wanting to leave any fingerprints at the scene the killer swaps the missing bulb with a new one being very careful not to leave any of his or her prints on the replacement bulb. I was passed out on the floor while the switch was being made. As I stated earlier, the Sunset Auditorium recently had a lighting overhaul and changed all of the bulbs to compact fluorescent bulbs designed to look like regular bulbs. I am on the Sunset Auditorium committee and we passed the motion to replace all of the bulbs at the same time, each one of these light bulbs is from the same manufacturer. The killer could not have been aware that the replacement light bulb would be different from any of the ones used in the Sunset Auditorium, at first glance they look the same. If the police check the light bulb in that stairwell socket, I believe they will find it not to be consistent with the brand of bulb used in this theater."

While all of the pageant participants were away, an emergency warrant was issued to search their hotel rooms. The police officers assigned to the search did not find Porsha's cell phone, but they did find the auditorium light bulb in one of the bedside lamps in the killer's room. The hotel uses a different brand of light bulbs from the auditorium; they do not have any fluorescent bulbs on their property. The killer swapped the hotel room bulb with the Sunset Auditorium bulb. Quite clever actually because there would be prints from the hotel staff on the bulb so it would not be completely clean. The police dusted the light bulb and discovered the killer's fingerprints all over it. The prints were matched against the police database for confirmation.

"Sheila didn't kill Porsha did she, Mr. Goodwill, you did!"

"What, I don't know what you're talking about!" protests Goody. Myrtle counters, "I think you know exactly what I'm talking about, it was your prints they found. It is my belief, Mr. Goodwill, that you killed the victim. I believe you lured Porsha to the side of the stage and killed her by pushing her down the stairs. You then attempted to cover your tracks by swapping the light bulb and casting suspicion on Sheila during your police interview. Viewgrove is a small town where most locals know each other and can usually identify who the visitors are. If you had tried to purchase a new light bulb from the general store there was a risk someone would have noticed you or you would have been captured on security camera. After all, why would a hotel guest need to purchase light bulbs? The best thing for you to do was to take a bulb from a place where nobody would see you. That place was behind closed doors in your hotel room. Police officers discovered the light bulb belonging to the Sunset Auditorium in your room, Mr. Goodwill. The officers checked with housekeeping and confirmed they had neither changed any bulbs in that room recently nor stocked that brand of light bulb. I came back to the Sunset Auditorium that night after everybody had left and I tried the light switch but it did not work. At the time, I did not know why. Right after discovering the light switch did not work, the killer attacked me. At some point last night, Mr. Goodwill picked up the victim's cell phone, perhaps when she fell, later that night, or some other time when everyone was distracted. You planted that cell phone on Sheila so she would be the one discovered with it and further confirm her as the killer. Perhaps Porsha found out about your police record and you were afraid she was going to tell people, I do not suppose that would go over well with the pageant organizers or your employer. Detective Chaplin contacted your employer and it turns out they have a zero-tolerance policy regarding misconduct against women. According to Human Resources, you would have been fired if they ever found out." Myrtle turns to address Goody directly, "The Police are waiting to arrest you for murder, you are going away for a long time Goody!" The crowd is left speechless. "He's all yours Detective." With that said, Myrtle turns to leave; she is late for her water aerobics class at the local YMCA.

Myrtle is actually late for her water aerobics class, she was not just saying that for the dramatic effect. She cannot survive on crime solving alone. Myrtle tends to get completely immersed in these cases, often times they keep her up at night or wake her up at strange hours. A few years ago she found that water aerobics helps her to relax and clear her mind. Water aerobics has become a group activity for her. When she first started, she did not know any of the retired women that took the class. Now through water aerobics, several of them have become some of her best friends. Although some of them no longer attend the class, they still all get together for lunch, shopping, and trips out of town. Last but not least, water aerobics gives Myrtle a chance to wear the cute bathing suits she loves to buy.

CHAPTER 25

Detective Zeus Chaplin takes over, "Officer Leighton, please release Sheila Johnson. I do apologize for the misunderstanding, Ms. Johnson." Sheila stands there still in shock and rubbing her wrists where the handcuffs had been. "Officer, please arrest Mr. Goodwill and charge him with murder. Don't forget to read him his rights." The look on Goody's face is of someone trapped in a room with the walls closing in. He looks as if he is contemplating making a run for the door but quickly realizes he would not get far. Goody slowly concedes it is all over and it is too much for him to take. He collapses in his chair. The officers quickly close in to take him into custody. During questioning at the police station, he breaks down and explains to Detective Chaplin what happened.

"Porsha confronted me and informed me Roxy had recognized me in the audience during the rehearsal a week ago. She said Roxy wanted to warn her I was here." Goody explained how he and Porsha had gone on a few dates, things did not end well, and she was well aware of his arrest record. Porsha asked him to meet her. Goody thought maybe she wanted to get together like old times but she wasted no time in proceeding to blackmail him. Porsha made it clear that if he did not agree to fix the pageant for her to win, she would contact his employer and let them know all about his past. "I have spent a lot of time and hard work reinventing myself and my reputation. If that information came to light, it would cost me my job at the auditing firm and at any other auditing firm for that matter!" Porsha gave Goody a few hours to think about it. The night of the murder, he asked her to meet him in the side stage stairwell to try to get her to change her mind. The stairwell is out of the way so there was little chance of being seen by the other contestants. Goody unscrewed the light bulb as an extra precaution, it would be dark so nobody would see them. When Porsha showed up he tried to convince her to reconsider but she would not. On top of winning the competition, she now wanted monthly payments too. He did not have that kind of money to pay her.

"Do you understand, she threatened to expose me to everybody in my city?"

Porsha would not listen to reason, he could not let her expose him, he would be ruined! Goody tried to talk her into giving him more time to think about it but she would not hear of it. The situation quickly escalated, she pushed him, and so he grabbed her and shook her just to try to scare her into changing her mind. She fought to break free of his grasp, lost her footing, and fell backward. After she fell down the stairs, Goody hid backstage until he could make his way back into the audience section. "What about the cell phone?" asks the Detective. "I never had Porsha's cell phone," replies Goody. He appears to have no idea who found the phone or how it ended up in Sheila's sweater. The first time he remembers even hearing about a cell phone is when Myrtle asked him about it in the initial police interview. He goes on to describe how he panicked and feared how this would look and what would happen to him. This was an accident but would anybody believe his story? Goody admits to being the one who attacked Myrtle after she interrupted him while he was switching the light bulb. He could not risk leaving a partial fingerprint as he tried to wipe off the bulb, or possibly breaking the bulb while trying to wipe it clean. "I had to switch the light bulb when that nosy old lady kept talking about the lighting system being recently upgraded."

Detective Chaplin maintains a straight face but he is not exactly sure what to make of any of this. He leaves Goody in the Interview Room so he can write out and sign his confession. Zeus takes a stroll down the hall to the soda vending machine. He still has to get used to saying soda, he grew up calling it pop. It is not even that he is thirsty, he just needs to do something while he processes what he has just heard from Goody. When Detective Chaplin first came to Viewgrove, the calls were mostly property line disputes, vandalism, and petty thefts. How things have changed, a few short years ago this type of crime was unheard of in Viewgrove. This was just another sign of the changing times.

CHAPTER 26

Porsha's mother and brother are scheduled to arrive in
town to identify and retrieve her body. Detective Chaplin
sends a squad car to meet the family at the train station.
The train is on time and the family arrives without
incident. They check into where they are staying and
schedule a time to go to the morgue. Detective Chaplin
makes a squad car available to transport them whenever
they are ready. Once they arrive at the morgue, their worst
nightmare is confirmed. The body is, in fact, Porsha, there
is no doubt about it. Until that time, there was always a
slim possibility in Porsha's mother's mind that it would
turn out not to be her. The officer transporting the family
expects to drive them back to their hotel but Porsha's
mother requests to be taken to the Sunset Auditorium
instead.

Ms. Marmalade had scheduled a time to meet the
family at the hotel, so she was surprised to see Porsha's
mother walk into the Sunset Auditorium. Ms. Marmalade

immediately expresses her condolences and informs them the pageant will be dedicated to Porsha's memory. All of the pageant contestants and staff members rally around the family to provide as much comfort and support as they can. The Pageant Director works with Porsha's family to organize a small memorial service to provide the contestants and pageant staff members a chance to share their memories of Porsha with the family and each other. After meeting Ms. Marmalade and visiting with the other contestants, Porsha's family insists on staying in town to watch the Ms. Plus-No Fuss pageant in honor of Porsha. Ms. Marmalade is glad to have them and adds two requests. The first request is that a portion of the Viewgrove show is dedicated to Porsha's memory. The second request is that the piece that Porsha would have performed for the talent portion still be performed during the show.

On the night of the pageant, everything goes especially well. Everyone works extra hard to make this the best show ever for Porsha. At the end of the talent portion, the show pauses and Ms. Marmalade takes the stage. After sharing Porsha's story with the audience, she asks for a moment of silence. The theater house lights dim while tea lights are lit all across the stage. The glow from the flames creates a warm ambiance and promotes a feeling of unity in the crowd. The moment of silence is followed by Porsha's mother being introduced. The crowd greets her with tears and applause as she walks across the stage to the main microphone. Everybody rises to their feet. Porsha's mother is visibly overwhelmed by the heartwarming reception. Sensing that she is ready to speak the crowd quiets down in anticipation. Porsha's mother takes a moment to thank everybody for their support, and also say a few heartfelt words about her daughter. The grieving mother takes a deep breath and closes her eyes. The stage microphone picks up her mother's breath as she exhales. She opens her eyes and begins to recite her daughter's poem. She had helped Porsha rehearse it so many times that she knew it by heart, although nobody would have faulted her if she had to read it. In that moment, it felt like they were reciting it together.

Mile in These Shoes (A poem for Porsha)

Any assumption about me,
Based on what you can see,
Will never come close,
To my actual reality.

My outward appearance,
Does not begin to describe,
Or start to tell the story,
Of what makes me so strong inside.

Life's wounds and bruises,
This outer shell hides,
My badges of honor,
That I now wear with pride.

I'm grounded in the knowledge,
That I'm more than equipped,
For great success in this life,
And deserve every blessing I get.

My confidence exudes,
The ignorance I excuse,
As I fearlessly cruise,
By those who try to abuse.

I stand proud and tall,
Succeeding despite it all,
See, you can never judge my blues,
Until you've walked a mile in these shoes.

The auditorium erupts in a roaring applause of approval. The noise was deafening. The size of the audience had tripled since news of the incident had gotten out. People have come out to support the family and the pageant because they either learned about it from a media outlet or heard about it from a friend. The Sunset Auditorium was sold out to supporters who were now all standing and applauding. It was a very moving scene, definitely a proud moment for the residents of Viewgrove. Ms. Marmalade was so overjoyed the pageant was such a big success. There had been major unforeseen obstacles in her path but somehow she had overcome them and managed to still put on a successful show. The audience was so impressed that they gave the whole cast a ninety-second standing ovation. Only Ms. Marmalade and a few others close to the situation knew how close the pageant came to being canceled. That all seemed like ages ago now, as she looked around at all of the local tv stations and reporters there to cover the event.

CHAPTER 27

Myrtle Jenson awakes in the middle of the night from her deep sleep, she is not surprised because this is nothing new. A lot of times after jury duty she has trouble sleeping because she constantly goes over everything in her mind until she is satisfied she has not missed anything. Catching criminals is something she takes very seriously. Playing a part in an innocent person being arrested is one of her biggest fears. She would be distraught if she ever learned that somebody she helped to convict was actually innocent. The room is pitch black but she finally sees everything clearly. She sits up in her bed and tries to determine if she will be able to fall back asleep or not. Trying to get back to sleep is a waste of time until she can clear her mind. Groping in the dark, her hand finds her cell phone charging on the nightstand. A push of a button and the phone comes to life displaying the time. Myrtle has to squint to focus while her sleepy eyes adjust to the brightness of the screen glow. As she suspected, it is nowhere near time for her to wake up. Now that Myrtle's eyes have adjusted a bit, she is able to see the remote control for the television. She clicks the button and the television turns on to the last channel she was watching. It happens to be a news replay that includes a story by local reporter Davina Roberts. Myrtle changes the channel and lands on another news recap with Ms. Roberts being interviewed about the pageant story. A little more than four hours have passed since the night of the pageant. The reporter, Davina Roberts was finally able to break the pageant story, per her agreement with Detective Chaplin. The story will be in the full twenty-four-hour news cycle. It is the feel-good story of the year so far. Davina shares with the interviewer how the story has been life-changing for her already and how people from high school and college that she has not heard from in years are reconnecting with her.

The Ms. Plus-No Fuss Pageant is being flooded with requests from cities wanting to be the next host location. The incident in Viewgrove turned out to be a bigger story than anyone could imagine, especially any of the residents. The local news picked up the story and it became a national story. Ms. Marmalade, Myrtle Jenson, Detective Zeus Chaplin, and anybody else associated with the pageant case became semi-famous and received numerous interview requests. Zeus Chaplin turned down all requests and only answered a few questions at the police press conference to close the case. Ms. Myrtle continues to ignore all news media requests for interviews and waits patiently for the news cycle to end so she can go back to her normal peaceful life.

With Zeus and Myrtle both declining to comment publicly, people hungry for details turn to the reporter Davina Roberts for comment. She has quickly become quite busy with all of the requests. She finds she actually enjoys the extra attention and having her name mentioned in the news. The managers at the Viewgrove Gazette are stepping all over each other to claim credit for her success. This story has made Davina a local celebrity and is she grateful for it. The only other person more grateful is Ms. Marmalade. Unlike Zeus and Myrtle, Ms. Marmalade gladly accepts all media requests for interviews. The spotlight comes to her so naturally that if you did not know better you would think she has been famous for years. She seems more than ready for this moment, this is finally her time in the sun. You will get no complaints from Ms. Marmalade, she is more than happy to get her fifteen minutes in the spotlight and shamelessly uses every bit of it to promote herself and her pageant. Myrtle and Ms. Marmalade did not get off on the best foot, but even Myrtle can see why people are inspired by her. Ms. Marmalade's personality is infectious, and it jumps right off of the television screen.

Myrtle watches yet another news outlet interview with Ms. Marmalade promoting her brand and declaring how she had a feeling this pageant would be a huge success. She was inspiring people to follow their dreams no matter what. Her story is an affirmation that anything is possible if you never give up. Ms. Marmalade has gained thousands of social media followers overnight. She started to receive texts, emails, and direct messages from people who felt inspired by her. As a result of all of the exposure, Ms. Marmalade has the Ms. Plus-No Fuss pageant booked solid through the next eighteen months. The pageant has never been booked that far ahead before. She is even able to raise all of her fees due to the demand. Business has never been this good, things are shaping up better than she could ever hope or dream. With the new success, Ms. Marmalade finally feels like all of her hard work and struggle is finally paying off. It gives her new motivation to keep working toward her dream of expanding and eventually franchising the pageant. One day there will be Ms. Plus-No Fuss Pageants in every state. The ultimate goal is to create a pageant large enough where contestants from around the world would compete for the title. It would be televised and watched by millions of viewers all over the world.

CHAPTER 28

The clock on Myrtle's car dash strikes seven as she arrives at the Viewgrove Gazette office. Her car pulls into the visitor parking lot and parks in the space closest to the building. The visitor parking lot is empty this early in the morning so Myrtle is free to pick any parking spot she likes. She exits her car and enters the building. At the front desk, Myrtle requests to see the reporter Davina Roberts. The desk receptionist asks Myrtle if Ms. Roberts is expecting her. Since the story broke Ms. Roberts has become one of the most requested people in the office. While many people have positive things to say, there are other people who have come down to the newspaper to voice their displeasure about how the story made their town look. There are small pockets of the local community that believe the article painted their town in a negative light and they do not appreciate the extra attention it has brought. For these reasons, the receptionist is very cautious about who she allows to schedule appointments with Ms. Roberts. Myrtle reads the concern on the receptionist's face and reassures her this is not a negative visit.

"Tell her Ms. Myrtle Jenson is here to see her."

The receptionist agrees to pass the message along. Myrtle watches her type on her keyboard, receive a response, and type some more. The receptionist looks up from typing long enough to advise Myrtle to take a seat. Good news, Davina has agreed to see her. Another ten minutes go by before Davina Roberts emerges to greet her uninvited visitor. Myrtle did not meet Davina on the night of the murder. She looks very different from that scrappy reporter that ran around the Sunset Auditorium hungry for a big break. That disheveled anxious reporter is gone. The woman Myrtle is meeting is polished and full of confidence. Davina is dressed in a beautifully tailored navy business suit with dark colored high heels. She is wearing light makeup, dark-rimmed glasses, and has her hair hanging down to her shoulders. Myrtle cannot help but be impressed.

"How are you doing Ms. Jenson, what can I do for you?"

Davina stretches out her hand to greet Myrtle. "You did such a wonderful job with your story. I just came by to congratulate you and see if I could buy you a cup of coffee?" replies Myrtle. Davina is curious what has brought Myrtle down to the office. It could be a follow up to the pageant story so she accepts the invitation. "Oh, that's very kind of you but I'm pressed for time, would you settle for a coffee out of the vending machine downstairs?" The coffee machine vends two cups of hot coffee and the ladies sit for a moment on a short bench directly across from the machine. "You did such an excellent job investigating the pageant story Ms. Roberts, may I ask how you initially learned of the incident?" Davina is so used to answering that question now that she goes into an automatic response. "First of all, thank you for the compliment. A good reporter does not reveal her sources, I hope you understand." Myrtle sees through this crafted response. "Yes, I understand," replies Myrtle. Davina changes her mind and no longer believes there is any new story or update to be learned from Myrtle. "Well, thank you for the visit and the coffee but I do need to be getting back to my office." Davina Roberts sees the disappointment on Myrtle's face. "Do you believe in fate Ms. Jenson? I've been a reporter for a while. I've investigated some really good stories during that time but none of them have brought me as much attention as this one. And to think it all started with an anonymous phone tip." Myrtle looks up with renewed interest.

"Wait, did you just say an anonymous phone call?" she asks.

"Yes, I happened to be the first person available when an anonymous call came in requesting to speak to a reporter. The caller said to hurry down to the Sunnyset Auditorium because there has been a serious accident involving a contestant in the big pageant." Myrtle listens intently. "Did this anonymous reporter by any chance have a woman's voice?" she questions. Davina Roberts thinks for a second before answering, "Why yes she did, how did you know that?" Myrtle smiles, "Oh, just a hunch," she answers. Davina continues, "Well, she called and requested a reporter come to the Sunset Auditorium to cover a big accident at a popular beauty pageant right away." Myrtle nods along before asking if she ever learned the identity of the anonymous caller? Davina is not one to reveal any of her sources, period. "I would have to protect my source if I did, but up to this point I have not learned her identity" answers Ms. Roberts, "I'm sorry but I really do need to be going now." Myrtle rises to leave, "Thank you so much for your time Ms. Roberts and continued success to you." Davina looks back and waves goodbye as she makes her way to the elevator. Myrtle assumes Davina is hurrying off to report another story or tape another interview, hopefully about something besides the pageant case. She reminds herself that everyone is entitled to their fifteen minutes of fame and they should get to enjoy it to the fullest, just as long as it is not obtained through a tragedy they caused. Myrtle waves back before reaching into her purse for her cell phone. The number is dialing as she walks out of the building to her car. "Hello, this is Myrtle Jenson, put me through to Detective Chaplin, it's important!"

CHAPTER 29

Myrtle meets Zeus at the Viewgrove Police Station. "Thanks for agreeing to meet me, Detective." After she briefs him, they both head off to pay Goody a visit. Goody is in jail while patiently awaiting his day in court. Myrtle is both surprised and relieved to find him still in Police custody. She thought perhaps he or somebody else would have posted his bail by now. Tracking down a bailed out Goody would have been a lot more difficult and not to mention time-consuming. For this case, time is the one thing they are short on. The iron gate buzzes open and an armed guard escorts Goody over to the table where Myrtle and Zeus are waiting for him. The look on his face says these are not the visitors he wanted to see.

"How have you been Goody?" asks Myrtle.

"What do you care!" he snaps.

"I just came by to tell you I'm headed over with the Police to have Wendy Ross or should I say Ms.

Marmalade arrested. We have good reason to believe she is leaving town today," answers Myrtle. "We know how she was the mastermind behind this whole thing. We are here to offer you a deal before she makes a deal and leaves you taking the blame for everything. We're giving you a chance to help yourself, Goody. You've been abandoned in a town you don't live in. Look around, nobody even cared to bail you out of prison. Ms. Marmalade is helping herself by getting out of town and leaving you here to face a murder charge."

Zeus and Myrtle leave the police station and race toward the hotel. The police squad car slices through traffic with the lights flashing and sirens blaring. Zeus pulls the police cruiser right in front of the hotel entrance and throws the gear into park. They both exit the vehicle and hurry through the front doors. There are a few Ms. Plus-No-Fuss pageant contestants in the lobby with their baggage waiting for taxis to the train station. The other contestants and assistants are still in their rooms packing and preparing to leave. This is the hotel where the contestants stayed for the week. The pageant participants in the lobby are not happy to see Myrtle and Zeus rush through the door. The clerk at the front desks looks up and welcomes them to the hotel. "Did you check out what I asked you to, Detective?" asks Myrtle. "Yes I did, and you were right," answers Zeus. The Detective approaches the front desk, flashes his police badge, and asks what room Ms. Marmalade is staying in. He and Myrtle ride the elevator up to Ms. Marmalade's floor. They exit the elevator and start down the long hotel hallway toward the room door. Myrtle cannot help but notice the renovations the hotel has completed since she has been there last. The interior has been completely updated, so much so that she would actually consider staying there now.

The long hallway is eerily empty, aside from a random room service tray sitting outside of a door. They arrive at the room number and Zeus knocks on the door with authority. The peephole goes dark before a voice behind the door asks who it is? "It's Detective Chaplin and Ms. Jenson ma'am, may we have a word with you?" Myrtle notices a shadow under the doorway approach and then retreat. "Who is it?", replies a voice behind the door. "She knows it's us, she looked through the peephole", whispers an irritated Myrtle. "Stay calm Ms. Myrtle, I noticed that too, let me handle this." The Detective knocks on the door again. "Ms. Marmalade, it's Detective Chaplin and Ms. Jenson, you need to open the door, we'd like to ask you a few questions?" They both turn their attention toward the creaking noise coming from the end of the hallway. False alarm, it is just another hotel guest leaving their room and heading toward the elevator. The guest smiles at them both before disappearing around the corner. A few of the other hotel guests crack their doors to see what is going on in the hallway. Myrtle asks Zeus if there is another way out of the hotel room. He assures her there is not, rooms this high up in the hotel do not have balconies, there is only one way in and out. At the same time, the room's occupant feels trapped and searches for a way out of the room even though she is sure there is not. Ms. Marmalade hurriedly pulls on the knob on the door to the adjoining room, but it is locked. The only way out of the room involves getting past the Detective waiting outside of the door. "One second," comes the reply. Ruffling sounds can be heard through the door along with the sound of zippers closing.

A few moments later the lock clicks and the door swings open.

"I'm surprised to see you two again," answers a shocked looking Ms. Marmalade.

"This feels like harassment Detective, I have a good mind to report you and your senior sidekick here to your superiors." Zeus is unfazed by the threat. "This won't take long ma'am, I wouldn't have come here if it wasn't important and necessary." Ms. Marmalade steps aside and swings the door wide enough to allow both Zeus and Myrtle to enter the hotel room. Myrtle follows behind Zeus just in case there is somebody waiting behind the door to knock them down. She is just starting to feel like herself again and does not want to risk another bodily attack. Myrtle's back aches just thinking about it.

CHAPTER 30

Once inside the room, Myrtle and Zeus can see there is luggage packed on the bed, zipped up and ready to go. If the two of them had arrived at the hotel any later they would have missed her for sure. The room appears clear of any other occupants so Zeus focuses back on Ms. Marmalade. "You're all packed here so I'll get straight to the point."

"I'm here to arrest you in connection with the murder of Porsha Jones."

"What are you talking about Detective, Goody committed that crime."

Myrtle steps in, "Oh yes, Goody committed the crime but we now know he wasn't acting alone. You planned the whole thing." Ms. Marmalade laughs in their faces. "Nonsense, Goody acted alone, I had nothing to do with it." Myrtle outlines what she believes happened. "I think the plan was to generate attention for the pageant by creating a scandal and having it become a huge news story, possibly going viral. You, Ms. Marmalade, had the most to gain from this whole thing. The financial success of the pageant was a deep illusion." Myrtle had requested Zeus Chaplin look into the pageant's financial records. "The police were able to uncover several creditor liens against the pageant, with that amount of money owed and the attendance numbers, it is doubtful the pageant could have survived much longer. Porsha was a known name in pageant circles. Since the story broke, the Ms. Plus-No Fuss pageant is booked solid and you have been able to secure tons of sponsorship money. You have become somewhat of a celebrity overnight. When we first met you, you told us the three people in the audience on that rehearsal night were strangers. You claimed you did not know any of them. I was watching Davina Roberts interview you on television and that is when it hit me. I had to ask myself, why would a Pageant Director have a feeling this pageant would be a huge success, Viewgrove is not a major city? Davina mentioned how people from her past had looked her up, but maybe she was not the only one that has happened to. I had Detective Chaplin do some additional research and it turns out you know Goody very well. The two of you went to college together. In fact, you were one of the people that filed that harassment suit against Goody before he moved and started over in another state."

"This sounds crazy, I have no motive," snaps Ms. Marmalade. Myrtle believes the opposite is true and she has lots of motive. "Ms. Marmalade, I believe you made a deal with Goody to create a news story to generate publicity and sponsorship income. You do not strike me as a killer, my thought is you planned for Goody to only injure a contestant, not kill one. I believe the same is true about Goody, I do not think his intent was to kill her. Either way, you were able to adapt to the new circumstances and still put your plan into action. Phone records will show that when you left Porsha's body with Goody that night, supposedly to get her emergency contact information, you really left to call in an anonymous tip to the newspaper reporter Davina Roberts. I went down to the Gazette office and spoke with Davina about that phone call. She remembers it very well because it was the beginning of her getting her big break. She specifically remembers the caller saying to come down to the Sunnyset Auditorium. A resident of Viewgrove is unlikely to mispronounce the name. There's only one person I know who refers to the Sunset Auditorium as the Sunnyset Auditorium and that's you. It's such a habit that I don't think you even realized that you said it wrong on that call. That's not the only call you made. You also called in an anonymous tip to Officer Leighton letting him know the missing cell phone was still in the auditorium. The investigation must not have been progressing quickly enough. You needed to cement Sheila as the killer so the show would still open on the scheduled night. At some point, you found that cell phone, didn't you? You had us concentrating our efforts on Goody, Roxy, and Sheila. That left you free to plant Porsha's cell phone in Sheila's sweater without detection. When the Detective and I first met you, you told us you would make your pageant a big deal and you did. If everything holds up you're on track to becoming a very rich woman. Goody is at the police station right now giving a statement. I believe you initially blackmailed him into agreeing to injure a contestant by threatening to expose his past. Once the contestant died, you struck a new deal with him, to keep him quiet. Maybe he was promised he would be bailed out of jail and made a partner in the Ms. Plus-No Fuss Pageant or something similar? It would have been much easier for Goody to avoid jail time had Porsha been injured instead of killed. Everything got a lot more complicated once Porsha died." "This is all speculation," snaps Ms. Marmalade, "You can't prove any of this." She starts to head toward her suitcases. "I suggest you get out of my way and let me leave before I sue you both for defamation of character and harassment!" Ms. Marmalade grabs her luggage and attempts to leave the room but she does not get far before Zeus stops her.

"Let me go, you have no reason to hold me!"

"Oh, but we do, we have every reason to hold you," answers the Detective.

Zeus explains how Goody got very nervous when he did not hear from Ms. Marmalade today. The Detective told him how Ms. Marmalade was leaving town today, and leaving him to face all of the charges. Myrtle concludes, "Once we explained to Goody what kind of jail time he was facing he was more than willing to cut a deal and fill in some of the details for us. Porsha was attempting to blackmail Goody but she did not realize she was playing right into his hands. The plan was to trip Porsha down the stairs with the intent to injure her just enough that she could not compete. It would make a compelling news story this year and an even bigger comeback story when she is invited back to compete in the pageant next year.

Goody expected her to twist an ankle or break a leg at the most. The two of you counted on Porsha remaining quiet on who tripped her because an investigation would reveal her attempted blackmail. She would say she tripped and fell on her own. The riddle of darkness has been solved, what was done in the dark has come to the light. You failed to account for reasoned action when choosing an accomplice. You have to consider Goody's attitude and norms when trying to predict his behavior. Goody is not a cold-hearted killer. This would have weighed too heavily on his conscious. He would have confessed and given you up eventually, regardless of what you tried to bribe or blackmail him with."

Myrtle ends with a personal message, "I have to say Ms. Marmalade, I actually enjoyed the pageant show you put on. I believe you are very talented, and I'm sure the pageant would have been a huge success in due time. Detective Chaplin will take you into custody when you're ready." Ms. Marmalade looks back toward Myrtle as she is being led out of the hotel room, "Could you do me a favor and tell the girls the next show has been postponed." Zeus Chaplin leads Ms. Marmalade out to the hallway. He allows Myrtle to exit the room before closing the door. "You do good work Myrtle, any chance you'd want to become an official police consultant?" Myrtle smiles, she has never considered becoming an official consultant, she is honored by the offer. "Let me think about it," she answers. Zeus turns back toward Myrtle and asks, "Can I give you a ride back to the station?" Myrtle thinks about it for a second, "No, I think I'm going to book a room here, I have some sleep to catch up on."

ABOUT THE AUTHOR

M. Malenga is an independent writer who lives and works in the United States. His advice for writers young and old is to never give up. "Every accomplishment starts with the decision to try" ~ Gail Devers.